12/16

THE ZANZIBAR SHIRT MYSTERY

AND OTHER STORIES

THE ZANZIBAR SHIRT MYSTERY
AND OTHER STORIES

BY
JAMES HOLDING

INTRODUCTION BY
JEFFREY MARKS

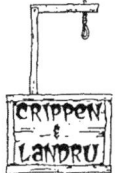

CRIPPEN & LANDRU PUBLISHERS
Cincinnati, Ohio
2018

Copyright © 1960, 1961, 1963, 1964, 1965, 1967, 1968, 1972 by James Holding
Copyright © 2018 (this edition) by John Betancourt.

All rights reserved. Printed in the United States of America. No part of this book may be used or reproduced in any manner whatsoever without written permission except in the case of brief quotations embodied in critical articles or reviews.

This book is a work of fiction. Names, characters, businesses, organizations, places, events and incidents either are the product of the author's imagination or are used fictitiously. Any resemblance to actual persons, living or dead, events, or locales is entirely coincidental.

For information contact:

Crippen & Landru, Publishers

P. O. Box 532057

Cincinnati, OH 45253 USA

Web: www.crippenlandru.com

E-mail: Info@crippenlandru.com

ISBN (softcover): 978-1-936363-26-1

ISBN (clothbound): 978-1-936363-25-4

First Edition: February 2018

10 9 8 7 6 5 4 3 2 1

Table of Contents

Introduction by Jeffrey Marks — 7
The Norwegian Apple Mystery — 11
The African Fish Mystery — 29
The Italian Tile Mystery — 43
The Hong Kong Jewel Mystery — 69
The Tahitian Powder Mystery — 83
The Zanzibar Shirt Mystery — 99
The Japanese Card Mystery — 115
The New Zealand Bird Mystery — 131
The Philippine Key Mystery — 151
The Borneo Snapshot Mystery — 169
James Holding Bibliography — 187

INTRODUCTION

James Holding was a late bloomer in terms of his literary career. Born in 1907 in Pennsylvania, Holding graduated from Yale in 1928, and worked most of his life in publicity and public relations at one of the world's largest advertising agencies Batten, Barton, Durstine, & Osborne in New York City.

His life's ambition was to be a published author. Aside from his advertising copy, Holding had written some light verse for the *Wall Street Journal* and humorous pieces published between 1924 and 1928 in the *Yale Record*, where Holding had served as editor during his tenure at the school.

In January 1959, at the age of 51, he decided to pursue his dream. He left the company, retiring from his position as Vice President and Copy Chief. He had earned a handsome nest egg to carry him to Social Security. He and his wife traveled the world, visiting parts of Africa and Europe, before returning to start his new career.

He achieved his dream the following year, when *Ellery Queen's Mystery Magazine* published a story. His first submission was rejected by the magazine, but he had another in the mail quickly. He started with a bang, publishing no less than seven short stories that year. His inaugural work, "The Treasure of Pachacamac" sold for $150. He followed that with a second sale to *EQMM*, a story he called "The Lady in A-12," which was presumably retitled for the magazine. Before the end of the year, he'd broken into *Alfred Hitchcock's Mystery Magazine* as well. He eventually sold more than 170 stories to *EQMM*, *The Saint*, *AHMM*, *Mike Shayne Mystery Magazine*, and other mystery magazines. His tales varied between the lighthearted cases of Hal Johnson, the Library Fuzz, to the grim exploits of The Photographer, a killer-for-hire, to a series in the classic sleuthing vein of Martin Leroy and King Danforth, mystery authors who wrote about their detective creation Leroy King.

If the name looks familiar, it was. The first name was a subtle variation of Ellery, and of course, King and Queen form the royal couple. Martin Leroy and King Danforth bore some resemblance to the two cousins, Fred Dannay and Manfred Lee, who wrote under the name Ellery Queen.

There are some potential clues to whom each character represented. Martin Leroy carried the same initials as Manny Lee. The two wives were Helen and Carol, compared to the real-life spouses of Hilda (Dannay) and Kaye (Lee,) which matches phonetically. However, the fictional character of Helen was matched with Martin, making for more confusion in any attempts to match characters to their real-life counterparts.

The stories had many differences from the cousins' real lives. Most obviously, the men shared a part of their name with their literary creation. Ellery Queen's name had been created using the given name of a childhood friend and the surname based on a playing card. Neither cousin had taken a round-the-world cruise. Both men would take their wives on cruises during their lives, but neither could afford the time away from writing to vacation more than 50 days. Holding, on the other hand, had traveled widely to Europe and Africa. Likewise, the interests of the characters are those that will drive the varying plots of the stories rather than using the true interests of the two collaborators.

The series took place over the twelve years with ten adventures, all of which are published in this collection. Since the couple and their wives are on an around-the-world cruise, the Nationality Object Mystery (from the early titles in the Ellery Queen series) could be easily employed. The series was not only reminiscent in the titles of Queen's Golden Age stories, the mysteries were clued, fair play mysteries set in foreign locales featuring amateur sleuths.

Since the series appeared in *EQMM*, the reader can assume that Fred Dannay enjoyed the stories. Sadly, there are no letters at Columbia University in Fred Dannay's correspondence on the magazine to corroborate this.

Holding's idea was unique at the time. While a number of books and book series have been published since that time with mystery authors serving as sleuths, he was one of the first to use real-life mystery authors as the detectives in a book. Since then, fictionalized authors have included Agatha Christie, Dorothy L. Sayers, Josephine Tey, Edgar Allan Poe, and Sir Arthur Conan Doyle. The writers of these stories featuring fictional versions of genuine authors used their real names, but there was no difficulty as they were deceased, but Holding used thinly disguised names of living authors.

Holding, who had a prodigious output of short stories, hired the Scott Meredith Agency to represent him in breaking in to novels. He signed a contract with Fred and Manny in 1961 to continue their young adult series, which had appeared between 1942 and 1954. The Ellery Queen Jr. novels featuring Djuna, the Queens' houseboy, had not kept up with the times. The books had been begun just after World War II and in the heat of the Cold War, the series and its small-town venue had begun to seem quaint.

Holding drastically altered the series. His first two books published in 1961 and 1962 in the rejuvenated series featured Gulliver Queen, the nephew of Ellery Queen. The series did not explain how Ellery had obtained a married sibling, but the changes didn't end there. The books varied from the former title structure of the original series of The Color Animal Mystery, which had begun with *The Black Dog Mystery*, to be The Mystery of the Adjective Noun, *The Mystery of the Merry Magician* and *The Mystery of the Vanished Victim*. Holding published a final Ellery Queen Jr novel in 1966, which reverted to using Djuna and the earlier title structure with *The Purple Bird Mystery*.

He followed those three works with other children's novels, but his forte was always the short story. He wrote for the major mystery magazines until 1988. The pinnacle of his career had occurred when his story, "A Decent Price for a Painting," which had appeared in *EQMM* in August 1982, received a nomination for a short story Edgar Award from the Mystery Writers of America. Sadly in the late 1980s, sales for his works dried up, and Holding lived another ten years without selling a work except for light verse to *EQMM* under the generic title of "Another Grave Tome." While this might have reflected a changing marketplace, it might have stemmed from the waning influence of the Scott Meredith Agency as well. Holding died in Pittsburgh in 1997.

Many of those later stories are still extant with his family, in the hopes that they might find a home someday, but his published stories remain a reflection of the variety of crime stories in the mid-twentieth century. While a number of Holding collections have appeared as Megapacks eBooks from Wildside Press, this book marks the first time Holding's works have appeared in print since their original publication.

Jeffrey Marks

The Norwegian Apple Mystery

Two hours after the stewardess found Angela Cameron lying dead in her bed in Cabin A-12, the news was all over the ship. That was pretty good going, even allowing for the fact that rumor is commonly conceded to fly faster on a ship at sea than anywhere else.

Most of the cruise passengers, of course, after forty-five days afloat, were eager for something besides shore excursions and shopping triumphs to gossip about; they seized this tidbit avidly, chewed it over, and passed it on to their neighbors with unusual celerity. Sunning themselves idly in the gaily striped deck chairs of the Norwegian cruise ship *Valhalla* as she plowed through the South China Sea toward Hong Kong, they chattered about Miss Cameron's death like a flock of hungry sparrows that suddenly discovers a slice of bread on the snow.

Despite the animation with which the passengers discussed the event, however, a general feeling of regret and even sadness spread with the news. For Angela Cameron had not only been vivacious, intelligent, pretty, and liberally endowed with sex appeal, she had actually been as well liked by the women passengers as by the men—which is saying a great deal for an attractive young woman traveling alone on a luxury cruise around the world.

The Danforths and the Leroys were sitting in the after Promenade Bar, having a pre-luncheon gimlet, when they were first apprised of the fact that there had been a death on board. As the bar steward leaned forward to deposit a dish of salted nuts on their table, he said to King Danforth in a solemn undertone, "Too bad about Miss Cameron, sir."

Helen Leroy, who was blonde, vital, and fast off the mark, spoke up before Danforth could say anything. "Miss

Cameron?" she asked of the steward. "What about her, Eric?"

"I'm sorry, Madam," the Norwegian bar steward said in his stiff English, "I thought you might have heard. Miss Cameron is dead. Edith, her stewardess, found her this morning. She died while reading in bed."

"Oh, dear, what a shame!" Carol Danforth said with instant sympathy. "She was such a lovely person. And how awful for Edith. What was it, Eric? Did Miss Cameron have a heart attack?"

"No, Madam," Eric said. "She choked to death on a bite of apple."

King Danforth and Martin Leroy exchanged glances. Death was no stranger to them. Indeed, they made a living from it. Under the pseudonym of "Leroy King," the two men operated with fabulous success as a writing team specializing in stories of murder, mystery, and crime. Several dozen best-selling novels, scores of short stories, numerous television and movie scripts about murder had made them world-famous. And here, on a cruise with their wives to get away from it all, the bar steward was saying—it might well have leaped directly from the page of one of their own mysteries—"No, Madam. She choked to death on a bite of apple."

Pressed by Helen and Carol, Eric gave them details. It was obvious that the story had swept through the ship's crew like a brushfire in the Hollywood hills. Miss Cameron usually had breakfast in her cabin. So Edith, her stewardess, unless warned away by a "Do Not Disturb" sign on the door of A-12, would normally enter Miss Cameron's cabin at ten o'clock, using her passkey, wake the lady, and take her breakfast order.

This morning, however, Miss Cameron had not awakened, nor did she need breakfast. Edith had found her clad in her nightgown, propped up against the pillows on her bed, a book fallen from one hand and a half-eaten apple from the other, her face dreadfully discolored and distorted, and her flesh beginning to turn cold. The reading lamp was still burning.

Although Miss Cameron was quite obviously past help, Edith had put through a hurried call for the ship's doctor. He was able only to confirm that poor Miss Cameron was indeed dead, and to point out the cause: a large fragment of the apple she had been eating was wedged tightly in her throat.

When the bar steward left them to their gimlets, Danforth wriggled his lanky frame in his chair, ran a hand over his crew cut, and said a trifle sheepishly, "I am not callous and unfeeling about things like this. But I couldn't help feeling that 'she choked to death on a bite of apple' would fit very well into one of our stories, Mart."

"I had the same thought," Leroy said, grinning. His dark eyes, short wide face, and compact body suggested Indian impassivity, but he denied it with every word and movement. "It was almost like being home again, working on a plot."

"Whoa!" Helen Leroy said. "This a vacation, remember? No plotting, no murder gimmicks, no looking for criminals to fit into stories—that was the agreement. Right?"

"Right," Carol Danforth agreed emphatically. She was short and dark, like her husband's partner, with a brisk way of speaking. "So forget about it. Miss Cameron died a perfectly natural accidental death—to coin a contradiction in terms. Let her alone."

"But what a starting point for a mystery!" Her husband's eyes kindled.

"The first thing we'd have to postulate," Martin picked him up instantly, "is that the girl did not die a perfectly natural accidental death, as Carol insists, but was murdered."

"Of course," Danforth said. "That's where the challenge lies. In figuring out how this perfectly natural accidental death could be made to appear that way by a murderer."

"And how he murdered her, and where, and why."

"Exactly."

"And who he was."

Their wives saw with resignation that the two incurable story plotters had the bit in their teeth and were not to be headed off. So rather than nag—and mellowed, moreover, by the gimlets they were drinking—they sighed and entered into the discussion.

"Before you apply your keen analytical brains to the solving of this murder that doesn't exist," Carol Danforth said, "do you realize that there are approximately seven hundred and fifty suspects aboard this ship? Four hundred crew members and three hundred and fifty passengers? Isn't that a few too many for even two geniuses like you to sift successfully?"

"Not at all," her husband said. "Motive. Surely all those people wouldn't have a motive for killing an attractive girl like Miss Cameron?"

"Not likely," Leroy agreed, "unless everybody on board found out Miss Cameron was a typhoid carrier, or fatally radioactive, or something like that."

Danforth shook his head. "Farfetched. Very few people would commit murder as a public service, even under such circumstances. No, it's got to be something more credible than that."

Helen Leroy said, "Well, I'm no writer, thank goodness, but if you want to be logical about it, I'd suggest that for one minute of respectful silence you turn your brilliant deductive powers on Miss Cameron's exceptionally fine figure."

King Danforth patted her hand and leaned back to sip at his gimlet thoughtfully. "Now we're getting somewhere, my sweet. A sex killing. That's more like it. This girl was very beautiful and, if you'll pardon a vulgarism, sensationally stacked. Suppose somebody made a pass at her, was ruthlessly repulsed, and killed her out of sexual frustration?"

"Hear, hear," Helen Leroy said. She was watching through the bar window the lazily lifting swells of blue sea that carried small antimacassars of lacy foam on their crests. "I'm getting bored with all the supposing. Doesn't that water look good enough to swim in?"

"Speaking of swimming," Danforth murmured, "the girl, Miss Cameron, was quite a fine swimmer herself. I have seen her churning back and forth in the ship's indoor swimming pool on occasion."

"In a bathing suit?" Leroy inquired.

"Of course."

"Then you're in a position to speak with authority on her figure, King. Was it enough to make a man commit murder?"

"It was," Danforth said appreciatively.

"This is the first I knew you'd been sneaking down to the pool to watch Angela Cameron do the Australian crawl!" Carol Danforth said sharply. "Luring husbands to swimming pools! No wonder she got herself murdered!"

"If you will be guided by my long experience as a plotter," Martin Leroy said hastily, "let us for the moment drop the motive and settle a few questions about method. She choked on an apple, remember."

"Easy," Danforth replied. "She was strangled first. The bite of apple was merely shoved down her throat by her murderer and wedged there for the doctor to find—so he would think exactly what he did think."

"Ah, but the bar steward said nothing about marks on the lady's throat that might indicate a manual strangling."

"The murderer didn't choke her with his hands. He garroted her."

"Impossible. A garrote cord would leave a plainly visible mark."

"Who said anything about a cord? The murderer used something soft to choke her—like a bed sheet or a bath towel."

"A bed sheet!" Helen Leroy laughed. "You men!"

"That would narrow down the suspects, though," Leroy grinned. "It ought to eliminate all the women aboard."

"Be serious," Danforth said with a frown. "This is a problem levity will not solve."

"All right. Where are we? We've got a resisting Miss Cameron strangled by a murderer, hypothetically male, using, say, a bath towel. Where do we go from there?"

"To lunch," Carol Danforth said grimly. "I'm starved."

"Don't anybody order an apple for dessert," Danforth said.

* * * *

Their table was in the *Valhalla*'s forward dining room, familiarly called the Runic Room. As they seated themselves for luncheon, they could tell from the buzz of conversation enlivening the usually sedate dining saloon that Miss Cameron's death was being discussed all about them. But adhering to their long-established rule that no business be discussed during meals—long-established by the wives—the Danforths and the Leroys talked about yesterday's shore trip to Bangkok, where they had been privileged to see the breathtaking temples, towers and cheddis of that holy city.

The cruise ship had anchored at dawn off the mouth of the Menam River, unable to enter because of the extensive sandbar that effectively blocks the entrance to oceangoing ships. A huge flat-bottomed barge, handled by Chinese seamen, had chugged majestically out to the *Valhalla* from shore, taken aboard almost all the *Valhalla*'s passengers, ferried them triumphantly over the sandbar, and three hours later disembarked them at the wharves of Bangkok, twenty-five miles up the river. The full day of sightseeing in 100-degree heat that ensued had been wearying, but worth it, they all agreed. It had been midnight when they climbed exhausted into their beds.

"That trip was rough enough to kill any but a hardened tourist," Leroy said. "I've never seen Helen so pooped as last night when we got back to the ship."

At this point Danforth broke their rule. He had been thinking about Miss Cameron reading in bed. "Everybody who took that trip to Bangkok was completely beat last night," he said. "And that makes me think Miss Cameron wouldn't have been reading in bed after she got back on the ship. She'd have been sleeping, brother—worn out like the rest of us."

"So?"

"So she must have been reading in her bunk this morning. Woke up early, say, couldn't get back to sleep, picked up a book, turned on her reading light, felt the pangs of hunger stir, reached for an apple, and took a bite. How's that?"

"That's fine. Monsieur Dupin, but where does it get us?" Leroy was saying when Jackson Powell, Thos. Cook's Shore Excursion Manager on the ship, came by their table on his way out of the dining room. He stopped for a moment.

"It's too bad about Miss Cameron, isn't it?" he asked. "Especially when she missed seeing Bangkok. She thought that would be the high spot of the cruise for her."

"What do you mean, she missed it?" Danforth exclaimed. "Wasn't she ashore yesterday with the rest of us?"

Powell shook his head. "She had a reservation for the shore trip, but she didn't go. I checked the list myself, and she wasn't there." He gazed morosely at the goat's cheese Leroy was applying to a cracker. "She'll never see Bangkok now," he said profoundly and walked away.

Later, as they left the Runic Room, Leroy grinned self-consciously. "Go on up to our regular deck chairs, will you? I'll join you on the Sun Deck."

"Where are you going, Martin?" Helen Leroy demanded.

"Got a small errand to attend to in the aft dining room."

"That's where Miss Cameron's table was," his wife said. "You can't fool me. Why don't you forget it, darling?"

"Just a notion I want to ask about. See you in the sun, kids." And Leroy took off.

* * * *

When he dropped into his chair on the Sun Deck five minutes later, Leroy was beaming. "I talked to her table steward. She didn't show up for any of her meals yesterday—or for dinner the night before!"

"Probably ate in her cabin," Carol Danforth said. "Can't we talk about anything else?"

But Danforth was muttering, "There's a way to find out." He left them, hurried down the starboard Sun Deck corridor to the elevator, and got off at A-deck; he and Carol occupied stateroom A-20. He went to his cabin, let himself in, and rang for Edith, the stewardess.

She knocked on the door a few seconds later.

"Come in, Edith," he said. She was a lovely statuesque Norwegian girl with auburn hair and an incredible snow-and-roses complexion. Her eyes were a bit puffy and red, Danforth noticed. "Sorry about Miss Cameron," he said sympathetically. "It must have been hard for you, finding her like that."

"It was not good," Edith said, making the "good" sound like "goot."

"Tell me, Edith. I hear Miss Cameron was not on the shore trip to Bangkok yesterday with us. And she didn't eat in the dining room yesterday or the night before. Was she in her cabin all that time?" The stewardess looked puzzled. "There is the 'Do Not Disturb' sign on her door all yesterday," she said, "and evening before. So I do not disturb her for dinner, breakfast, or luncheon. That is how I am told, when there is the sign 'Do not Disturb.' Let her alone, yes?"

He raised his eyebrows. "So she stayed in her cabin all that time, even when she was supposed to be on a shore excursion to Bangkok?"

"Not all the time," Edith corrected. "At five o'clock in the afternoon, yesterday, I use my key and enter Miss Cameron's cabin. I am worried. I have not seen her since the afternoon before yesterday."

"And?"

"She is not in A-12. Nobody is there."

"Oh. And the bed, was it made up? Had it been slept in?"

"It is made up, although I have not made it up since morning before yesterday."

Danforth said, "She probably made it up herself yesterday. Slept so late she hated to bother you, maybe. Was her door locked when you went in yesterday?"

She nodded.

"And how about this morning when you—er—discovered her?"

"Not locked," the young stewardess said, obviously picturing in her memory how it had been. "Her door key is on the dressing table beside the fruit tray."

"And was the 'Do Not Disturb' sign gone from her door?"

"Yes."

"Did you touch her when you found her this morning?"

"Yes. Her arm when I shake her." Edith shuddered. "She is getting—she is getting—"

"Cold?"

Silently, she nodded.

"But still a little warm, too?"

"Still a little warm. But more colder. Colder than warm."

Danforth said, "Thanks, Edith. Mr. Leroy and I write stories about things like this, you know? We're always interested in how such things happen. And we liked Miss

Cameron very much."

"She was nice," Edith said and left quickly.

* * * *

Helen, Carol, and Martin were waiting for Danforth in their Sun Deck chairs when he returned, but not with any noticeable eagerness, because all three of them had dropped off into the well-fed, sun-induced post-luncheon nap that overcame most of the passengers regularly every afternoon.

King was hurt. "Hey!" he said loudly, sitting down in his deck chair.

They awoke with a simultaneous start.

Helen Leroy yawned. "You're back, King. Wish you'd stayed longer. I could have milked another half hour out of that nap."

"Listen—" Danforth began eagerly.

"Oh, shut up, darling," Carol Danforth said. "We're all exhausted. Go away somewhere else and plot your plans, or vice versa. Helen and I have had it."

"Not me!" said Leroy. "What's the good word from your recent investigation, King? You've been interviewing Edith, I assume."

"You assume right. Miss Cameron spent yesterday and the evening before in some mysterious limbo, Mart. She was not ashore in Bangkok. She was not in the dining room for any meals, as you yourself confirmed. And she was not in her cabin!"

"Not in her cabin?" his partner repeated, astonished.

"Edith says no. A 'Do Not Disturb' sign was up all day yesterday and the evening before. But Edith looked in at five yesterday. No Angela."

"What do you know!" Leroy breathed. "Now there's a nice complication."

"It's nice complications that make the yarn," Danforth said sententiously. "So...where was she?"

"With the murderer," Leroy suggested. "Shacked up in his cabin while she repulsed his advances."

"Huh-uh. All the able-bodied men among the passengers were in Bangkok."

"The crew. It was obviously a member of the crew. They didn't go to Bangkok."

"True. They didn't."

They sat thinking in silence, watching the faint black stream of cinders from the *Valhalla*'s single stack go streaming away to port in the light breeze. Then Danforth said calmly, as though there had been no hiatus since his last remark, "The girl was murdered the day before yesterday. That would explain everything."

"The day before yesterday!" Leroy protested. "Impossible! The bar steward distinctly told us that Angela Cameron was just getting cold when Edith found her this morning. Beginning to get cold, I believe Eric said. They don't stay warm for thirty-six hours, Mastermind!"

"Yes, that is a problem. In Edith's own words, 'Miss Cameron had still a little warm, but more colder.'"

Silence once more.

Leroy suddenly said, "The average rate of body-cooling is more or less one degree per hour, depending on the surrounding temperature and moisture."

Danforth looked at him respectfully. "You're quoting," he said. "But from what?"

"The Encyclopedia Britannica, I think. Or is it our own *The Swedish Match Mystery*? I don't remember. But I read it somewhere."

"So where," Danforth queried, "could a dead girl be stashed on this ship where the surrounding temperature and moisture might retard the cooling of her body?"

"The refrigerator," Helen Leroy said drowsily.

"Not the refrigerator, bright girl," her husband's partner denied. "That's where she is now. We want just the opposite effect."

Leroy had a faraway look in his eyes. "Friends," he announced, "I believe I've come up with the answer."

"Which is? And don't be so darn smug!" his wife exhorted him.

"Why, the natural, the obvious, the only possible place."

Danforth said, "Don't tell me. Let me guess. The steam room down on D-deck beside the swimming pool."

"Bingo! The steam room, of course. Where else?"

"Of course!"

Again silence descended upon the plotters.

This one lasted longer. But eventually Danforth broke it. "Say. The steam room is right off the swimming pool, next to the massage room. Miss Cameron was a regular swimmer in the pool each afternoon. In that very revealing suit. Somebody down there fell for her, but hard. Right?"

"You ought to know," his wife said.

"Somebody who saw her in that suit so frequently that he simply couldn't go on resisting his baser impulses. So the day before yesterday—"

"Hold it, King, hold it." The interruption was Leroy's. "You keep trying to put the finger on somebody for this fictitious crime. I say we've got to work out how it happened first. Explain to me, if you please, the bit about the steam room. I've been in it. I've steamed myself like a soft shell clam with sinus trouble. I've lost six pounds in that room. But where could anybody hide a grown-up girl's body in that Spartan chamber?"

"Close your eyes, Mart," Danforth chortled. "Conjure up a picture of that steam room. It's got open framework wooden benches in it, like bleacher seats in a ball park, for the customers to sit or recline on while steaming themselves thin. Correct?"

"Correct."

"Now think about the space behind those benches."

"Got it."

"Do you see?"

Leroy opened his eyes. "You're right. There's a space behind the benches about a foot and a half wide, backed by the wall of the steam room. And the back wall is solid. A body dropped in there would be hidden."

"Exactly."

"Hidden from the customers, unless somebody happened to climb to the top row and look straight down the back."

"And the steam room wasn't used by more than a dozen people yesterday, remember. Most of us were ashore in Bangkok."

"Right!"

"So there's where the murderer kept Angela Cameron," Danforth said, "between the time he killed her and early this morning."

"When did he kill her, Swami?" Carol asked, in spite of herself.

"The probabilities seem fairly clear. What time does the indoor pool close?"

"Six o'clock."

"And Miss Cameron liked to do her swimming late in the afternoon, as I observed. Therefore, she probably went for her usual swim about five-thirty, day before yesterday. She swam until the pool closed. By then she was doubtless the only person left down there, aside from the staff. When she went into the ladies' dressing room to take off her wet suit and put on her robe—that's when it happened. The murderer, who had been waiting for just this opportunity, tried for his home run and got thrown out at first. That's when he killed her, to keep her from screaming the ship down or reporting him to the Captain."

Leroy picked it up. "And then he put her in the steam room. The intense heat and moisture in there retarded, as you so delicately phrased it, the cooling of her body until the killer could get it back up to her cabin early this morning."

"Just a moment." Danforth raised a magisterial hand.

"Why would he want to delay having her body found for a whole day?"

"Sheer terror of discovery, I should think," Carol said, now in it all the way.

"Perhaps he hoped to obscure the time of her death by allowing the mad confusion of the Bangkok shore excursion to intervene," Helen said.

"There could have been any number of reasons. The important thing is," Leroy said, "the killer stashes Angela behind the steam room benches, then casually goes up to A-deck and drapes a 'Do Not Disturb' sign on her cabin door."

"He knows her cabin is A-12 from the tag on her door key."

"Yes. And he hangs out the sign to stall, to give him time to think, to plan."

"Check. But how does he get her body up to her cabin again, early this morning?"

"Maybe in a hamper of dirty towels from the swimming pool? The body covered up by laundry?"

"Perfect. He folds her body into a wheeled hamper, covers her with some soiled towels from the dressing rooms, and wheels her up to her cabin—pretending he's collecting laundry. And with no one stirring except crew members so early in the morning, he'd find it easy to wheel the cart right into her cabin at the proper moment. And out again, later."

"Not a very original method of body transport. But it could work."

"Of course it could work. Let's see, now. Edith said the door was locked yesterday afternoon when she went in and saw that Angela was missing. But it was not locked this morning when she discovered the body. What about that?" Danforth waited for suggestions.

Helen came through. "She had her room key with her when she went down to swim, naturally. So the murderer simply used her own key to get into A-12 when he took the body back."

"Very good. And why wasn't A-12 locked this morning when Edith discovered the body?"

Leroy said, "Because the killer had no way of locking the door after him when he left her cabin! They're not snap locks. And he had to leave her key inside the room because that's where it would naturally be when Miss Cameron was in her room. He couldn't take a chance that a missing key might arouse suspicion."

"Not bad," Danforth said. "That could be it."

Leroy sighed wistfully. "We could make an interesting story out of this, King, if we gave it the proper treatment. I particularly like the bath towel touch. Victim strangled with bath towel, then concealed under same when wheeled to stateroom in laundry cart."

"And then," Danforth went on, ignoring him, "What happens? He's in her cabin now, with the body-laden cart. I say he dresses Miss Cameron in her nightie, puts her into bed, props her up, turns on the reading lamp, arranges a book near one hand, the apple near the other—and then scrams."

"Having first bitten a piece out of the apple and wedged it far down her throat." Leroy nodded. "I like it, King, I like it."

"So who's going to suspect murder? It's an accident. Anyway, the killer comes out of A-12 with his cart and goes about his normal business, which is obviously merely the taking of some soiled towels to the ship's laundry."

"The stairway down to the laundry is on A-deck, aft," Leroy said. "That fits."

"And poor Miss Cameron is found this morning at ten, dead in her bed, having choked to death on a bite of apple sometime during the night or early this morning. The victim of what my dear wife calls a perfectly natural accidental death." Danforth leaned back and lit a cigarette.

"There we are. No holes in that fabric."

"But," said Helen Leroy.

"Are there buts?" King Danforth asked, "Do you mean there are loose ends?"

"One," she said succinctly. "Who's the man who couldn't resist his baser impulses when he saw Miss Cameron in a bathing suit?"

Danforth laughed. "You do have a point there," he said. "What do you think, Mart?"

"I am at an extreme disadvantage in this area of speculation," Leroy said. "I am not a swimmer." He slanted a look at Danforth. "I am not even drawn to swimming pools by sensational chassis, either singular or plural. In fact, I have never been down to D-deck for anything except a steam bath and massage. But if I were to pick out a member of the crew who could have fallen for Miss Cameron's charms at the swimming pool and killed her when he was denied them, I am in favor of that Neanderthal blond Viking type with the rabbit's teeth who's employed to pull you out of the pool if you start to drown. Isn't his name Nils?"

"The very fellow I was thinking of," Danforth agreed. "And he'd have ready access to the towels, too."

"And the laundry cart," Helen Leroy said. "But I know Nils quite well. He's sweet."

"Perhaps your chassis is not sensational enough to arouse the beast in him," her husband started to say, but thought better of it.

"Well," Danforth said, "if fact were as strange as Leroy King's fiction, which it unfortunately ain't, that's the way poor Angela Cameron would have got hers."

"Face it," Leroy sighed. "Miss Cameron just had the bad luck to choke to death on her apple. And to be quite fair to Nils, the lad at the swimming pool, I'd say that if he went to an orthodontist and got those outboard teeth of his brought into line, he'd be better-looking, more appealing, and more gentle than either gentlemen in this present company."

"That," Carol Danforth said heartily, "is fact, not fiction!"

* * * *

At dinner they were in high spirits and ordered a bottle of champagne. "To celebrate," Leroy said, "our solution of The Norwegian Apple Mystery."

They had stingers on the rocks in the ballroom after dinner, while playing Bingo games which were always won by other passengers. Then they danced until midnight to the excellent music of the all-Scandinavian jazz band.

And when they finally descended to their cabins on A-deck to turn in, they were pleasantly aware of the fact that despite its tragic result for one of their fellow-passengers, the day had been stimulating.

To get to their staterooms from the elevator, they had to pass the door of Cabin A-12, recently occupied by the late Miss Angela Cameron. As they approached it, the door to A-12 opened and Edith, their stewardess, stepped out into the corridor, carrying a fruit tray. She bobbed her auburn head at them and started to pass. Danforth put out his hand and restrained her.

"Hi, Edith," he said. "Something more happening in A-12?"

"No, Mr. Danforth," she said. "I am cleaning up Miss Cameron's stateroom, packing her things. To take off the ship with her when we arrive Hong Kong. It is now all finished. Her parents radio to have her cremated in Hong Kong, and send ashes home on airplane."

"Poor thing," Helen Leroy said, suddenly feeling very guilty. But then she looked at the dish of fruit that Edith was taking from A-12 to dispose of in her service pantry.

Leroy was looking at it, too. He reached out and took an apple from the tray. "Is this the apple Miss Cameron was eating when she choked?"

Edith nodded.

"Look at that," Leroy whispered.

He held out the apple.

The flesh of the apple had turned brown where someone had taken a single large bite out of it.

The tooth marks showed clearly along the top edges of the bite. They could not possibly have been made by the small even teeth of Angela Cameron. Unmistakably, they had been carved into the fruit by two very large, protruding front teeth.

The African Fish Mystery

It was merely a chance remark of their driver's that led to what King Danforth and Martin Leroy later described as one of the most stimulating exercises in deduction they were privileged to enjoy during their entire round-the-world vacation trip with their wives. And unlike The Norwegian Apple Mystery it was not a case of sudden death that precipitated their discussion, but a case of sudden wealth—which, as any good gossip columnist can tell you, is far from intriguing.

The two mystery-story writers, known to millions of fans simply by their collaborative name of "Leroy King," had left their cruise ship *Valhalla* at Cape Town and embarked with their wives on an inland tour of Southern Africa by car, intending to rejoin their ship at Durban. And they were sixty miles out of Pretoria on the smooth road to Machadadorp when their driver, Ralph Muir, making idle conversation, remarked to King Danforth in the front seat beside him, "I hope you'll turn out to be as lucky as a passenger I drove earlier this year, Mr. Danforth."

"How's that?" Danforth asked.

"When we got back to Johannesburg from the trip I drove him on, he came into a great fortune and went home to live in England."

"I could stand the fortune," Danforth said wryly, "but Scarsdale is okay with me."

"What was his name?" Carol Danforth inquired from the back seat. Her dark eyes sparkled with interest.

"A Mr. Duke Carrington," Ralph replied.

"Duke." Helen Leroy laughed. "That puts him a little lower in the scale of royalty than you are, King."

Leroy nudged his lovely blonde wife and grinned. He was

small and dark and intense. "Don't flatter King, dear," he urged. "He's all but insufferable now." But there was affection in his voice.

Carol said idly, "What kind of fortune, Ralph?"

"Some relative in England," said Ralph, "died and left Mr. Carrington a large estate. There was a letter of notification waiting for him when we got back to Joburg. Everybody in town was talking about his inheritance within a day or two."

"A likely story," Danforth said idly, too. "I suppose he mentioned his rich relatives to you during your trip together?"

"No, he didn't," Ralph said. "On the contrary, I gathered the impression he was quite alone in the world."

Leroy squinted out the side window at three almost naked black children who were patiently watching over a herd of cattle beside a gaily decorated Ndebelc village. "Tell me, Ralph," he said. "Did Mr. Carrington seem very flush after you got back to Johannesburg?"

"He was the talk of the town," Ralph said. "Living very high off the hog, for him. I understood the solicitors in England advanced him a bit of his legacy."

Danforth turned his head and met Leroy's eyes. He rubbed a speculative hand across his crew-cut. "Are you thinking what I'm thinking, Mart?"

Leroy grinned. "I am. Was there ever a hoarier chestnut than the sudden wealth bit after taking a trip somewhere?"

"Please watch your language, Martin," Helen said with dignity.

He ignored her. "We've used it ourselves, King, a dozen times. In The Color of Blood and The Baronet's Bullet, to mention only two."

Carol pretended to groan. "Here we go again," she said. "More plotting by the world's champions. Are we in for another busman's holiday, Helen?"

Leroy said penitently, "We'll forget the whole thing, Carol. Fishy as it sounds, eh, King?"

"Fishy as it sounds," Danforth agreed solemnly.

"It doesn't sound fishy to me," Helen said. "What's fishy about a man inheriting a fortune? Happens all the time."

"So soon after taking a mysterious trip? And telling people ostentatiously that he has suddenly become the lucky heir of some vague relative in England?"

"Why not? Anyway, there wasn't anything mysterious about the trip, was there, Ralph?"

Muir grinned. "Not a thing."

At this point the black sedan in which they were traveling breasted the slope of one of Africa's rolling green hills, and the engine sputtered for a moment, misfiring several times before resuming its purr of power.

"Whoops," Danforth said. "A fouled spark plug."

Leroy said, "Sounds like a little dirt in your carburetor, Ralph. Or your gas line."

Carol said, "For my money, we're about to run out of gas."

"It's nothing to worry about," Ralph reassured them. "Happens every once in a while, like a chronic cough. There's nothing wrong with the plugs, carburetor, or feed lines that I can find. And we aren't running out of petrol, cither, Mrs. Danforth. If we do, I have an extra five-gallon can stowed in the boot. So rest easy."

"All right," Carol said. "But I'm sorry Mr. Duke Carrington's fortune was a phony."

"Who said it was a phony?" Leroy protested.

"All we imply is," Danforth said, "that the inheritance gag was a phony. Not the fortune."

Carol sighed with mock resignation. "Well, go ahead and figure it out. Helen and I will sit here and admire your cerebration along with the scenery."

Leroy leaned forward and tapped Danforth on the shoulder. "Begin, my dear fellow," he said encouragingly.

"Very well," Danforth said with a quick smile that made his battered features very attractive. "First, Ralph, did Mr. Carrington take the same trip we're taking? Johannesburg, Pretoria, Kruger Park, Hluhluwe, and so on?"

"Oh, no. It was a different trip entirely—not a regular tour like yours." Ralph looked through his windshield into the sunny distance of the high veldt, and his eyes took on a reminiscent gleam. "My instructions were to pick up Mr. Carrington at the Carlton Hotel in Johannesburg and drive him anywhere he wanted to go for as many days as he paid the car hire. I was to take a tent, sleeping bags, mosquito nets, and some food supplies in case he wanted to camp out in the bush as we went along."

"Camp out? Then I suppose you drove a Land Rover or Jeep?" Leroy suggested.

"No. We drove this car. He didn't expect to get into really trackless country."

"Where'd you go?" King asked.

Ralph said, "It turned out to be a fishing trip. Mr. Carrington told me to keep as close to the Vaal and Orange Rivers as the roads allowed, as far as the mouth of the Orange, while he did a little river fishing. Something he'd wanted to do ever since he'd been in South Africa."

"Pardon me if I parade a bit of erudition," Danforth said, "but there's something slightly fishy with that fishing story, I think. According to a large pamphlet on the Transvaal I recently read, there's much better fishing in any number of places than in the Vaal and the Orange."

Ralph shrugged. "I was told to drive him anywhere he wanted to go."

Leroy said, "Did Mr. Carrington go fishing every time you camped near the river?"

"Yes, if he thought it a likely spot."

"Did he stay long at any one place?"

"No. We did our regular hundred and fifty to two hundred miles a day in the car. Mr. Carrington only went fishing after we stopped for the night."

"I see," Leroy said. "Or rather, I don't see. Why all the rush to make two hundred miles a day, just for a couple of hours' fishing in the evening?"

"We had a long way to go," Ralph explained patiently, thinking his American passengers a strange lot. "The mouth of the Orange is nearly a thousand miles from Joburg."

"Why," asked Helen, "go so far—just to fish in the evenings?"

Ralph shrugged again.

Danforth asked, "What did this Carrington do for a living? Did he have a job?"

"Yes," Ralph said, skillfully nursing his car through another small fit of chronic coughing, "in Johannesburg. He worked at one of the gold mines on the Rand."

"Ah," Leroy said complacently. "Gold. Makes you think, doesn't it?"

"It does," said Danforth. "It makes me think that perhaps Carrington was mixing some gold prospecting with his fishing. And struck it rich."

Ralph entered into the spirit of the game. He shook his head. "I don't think so, Mr. Danforth," he said. "He never brought any ore samples back from the rivers. Just fish."

"The absence of ore samples wouldn't mean anything," Leroy muttered. "Not if he was looking for placer gold. That he would find in the river itself—in the form of nuggets or dust."

That sounded quite logical to Helen. "I'm proud of you, dear," she complimented her husband. "And now that we've got that settled, let's stop for lunch some place before I suddenly starve to death before your eyes."

"Only a few more miles to Machadadorp," Ralph promised. "We can eat there, at the Hydro-Baths Hotel. It's very pleasant."

When they re-entered the car after an excellent luncheon, Danforth was clutching a large Mobilgas road map of South Africa. And having exchanged places with Leroy at the noon break, he now sat between the girls in the back seat.

He spread his map and studied it conscientiously for several miles as Ralph Muir headed the car down the road to Nelspruit and White River. Finally, Danforth addressed his partner blandly, "You were saying, Mart, that perhaps Mr. Carrington discovered a pocket of placer gold while fishing?"

"Could be," Leroy said.

King said, "It occurs to me that a gold prospector—supposedly Carrington in this instance—always uses a miner's pan of some sort to separate the gold from the river gravel?"

Leroy nodded thoughtfully. "Ask him," he said magnanimously. "You thought of it."

Danforth said, "Well, Ralph, did your Mr. Carrington have, among his personal effects, a miner's pan or batea, as I believe the device is sometimes called?"

Ralph said, "Sorry to disappoint you, but no. Not a sign of one."

"There goes an excellent theory," Leroy mourned.

"However," Danforth persisted, "I have another avenue to explore with Ralph that may prove productive."

Carol said, "Move your map a minute, darling, so I can see out the window. We're coming to orange groves, I think. How heavenly!"

King folded the map obligingly. "Ralph, did you actually reach the mouth of the Orange River?"

"We did, sir. And stayed there for four days. Camped on the south shore of the outlet. Mr. Carrington fished and I loafed."

"Was the fishing very good?" Danforth asked.

"It wasn't anything special," Ralph replied.

Danforth took a deep breath. "Didn't it strike you as

peculiar, Ralph, that Carrington should want to drive two hundred and fifty miles out of the way merely to reach the river's mouth where, by your own testimony, the fishing was nothing special? And then should want to stay there four days?"

Ralph looked a bit taken aback. Leroy said, "What do you mean, 'two hundred and fifty miles out of the way'?"

"The map shows no auto roads along the Orange River west of Pella," Danforth explained. "The only way you can get near the river's mouth by car is to take a big detour south through a town called Springbok, and then north again along a dead-end coast road to the place where the Orange empties into the Atlantic."

"And thank you, Mr. Lowell Thomas," Carol murmured admiringly, rolling down the car window the better to sniff the delicious fragrance of orange blossoms that permeated the countryside.

"That's right, Mr. Danforth," Ralph admitted. "That's exactly the route we took."

King said, "Are you sure Carrington did nothing but fish at the river's mouth? It seems evident to me that he went there for some other purpose."

Ralph insisted. "I had him in view practically every minute. He favored the inside of the sand bar that lies across the river's mouth, and since the river was low, he'd stand on the pebble beaches of the small islands that stud the river's mouth and cast from there. By the hour. The water was quite shallow."

Suddenly Leroy, in the front seat, reached back a hand demandingly. "Lend me your map, King." He took the map, opened it, frowned down at it for a moment, then folded it with a flourish. "I begin to see daylight," he said softly. "But Ralph gave me the lead."

"Me?" asked Ralph, surprised.

"Your mention of pebble beaches has awakened the sleeping giant that is my brain. Harken." He paused, as though to let them hear his brain whirring. "Girls, what is Africa famous for besides gold?"

"Elephants," Carol replied promptly.

"Not elephants. Something more precious."

"Lions," Helen said. "I think they're precious."

"By Jove!" Danforth exclaimed. He leaned forward to pat Leroy approvingly on the back. "I believe you're right! Diamonds, of course."

"It has to be diamonds," Leroy said.

"A girl's best friend," said Helen with enthusiasm. "Let us start immediately for the mouth of the Orange River. If there are diamonds there, I want to go fishing with Duke Carrington!"

"King Solomon's Mines!" Carol offered. "Is that where they were?"

Leroy shook his head. "The other direction, Carol. Sheba's Breasts, the mountain peaks that Rider Haggard described as marking the spot, are supposed to be in Swaziland, I believe."

"Talk about parading erudition," Helen said, "you do collect some of the oddest information, darling!"

"Anyway, Rider Haggard only dreamed up King Solomon's Mines to prove he could write a more exciting story than Stevenson's Treasure Island," Danforth commented. "Please, ladies, look at the scenery for a bit while your husbands handle this matter of the diamonds in an orderly fashion. Martin?"

"Where," Leroy asked didactically, "are the most famous diamond fields of Africa?"

"Kimberley."

"Right." Leroy sighed happily and handed the map to Danforth. "Look where the Vaal River flows."

Danforth looked. "Why, of course! Close to Kimberley."

"Within a few miles. And it's not too much to believe, is it, that the Vaal might wash some diamonds out of the earth it flows through, and carry them with it as it joins the Orange River?"

"And the Orange carries them right along to the ocean!"

"Head of the class. There must be deposits of diamonds at the mouth of the Orange River. Not gold. Diamonds."

Ralph Muir spoke up. "Alluvial deposits? Nothing new about them. For three hundred miles along the coast of South West Africa, they've been working open-pit alluvial diamond mines for years."

"I didn't know that," Leroy said. "But actually it helps our theory. There are diamonds washed to the coast by rivers. And Carrington, being a knowing fellow—perhaps a mining engineer?—figured he might pick up some loose diamonds on the island beaches where the Orange meets the sea."

"Mixed with the pebbles, eh?" Ralph chuckled. "I suppose it's remotely possible." He looked at the writers curiously. "That never occurred to me," he said, "and I live here."

Leroy was modest. "You have to have a feeling for these things."

Danforth said, "It takes a special kind of mind," and grinned at his partner. "Let's see how the diamond theory stands up under searching scrutiny. Ralph, did you notice that Carrington stooped frequently while fishing the mouth of the Orange?"

"When he wanted to change lures or take a fish off the hook, he'd squat on the beach. Naturally."

"And picked up diamonds," Helen said. "Some fish!" She wrinkled her nose. "But wait. Can you tell a rough diamond when you see one?"

Ralph answered that. "Yes, you can. They're usually rather rounded and greasy in appearance, greasier than a pebble. With maybe one flat side." He began to smile broadly and Leroy noticed it.

"What's funny?"

"Nothing, really. I was just remembering that the Star

of South Africa, a fabulous diamond, was found on the bank of the Orange River."

"Why didn't you mention that sooner?" Leroy grinned.

"Never thought of it. Back in the seventies, just after it was found, there were ten thousand prospectors along the banks of the Orange and the Vaal, I've heard. But that's all over now."

"Not for Carrington," Danforth said. "He picked up a fortune in diamonds. And he disguised his trek to the river mouth as a fishing trip to keep you from knowing what he was really up to. When he got back to Johannesburg, he probably disposed of a diamond or two on the black market to celebrate his good luck, then circulated the inheritance story to account for his sudden wealth."

"But why all the secrecy?" Helen protested. "Why not tell the world about his diamond windfall?"

"Probably wanted to come back for more diamonds if he ever went broke," Danforth speculated. "Didn't want anybody to know where he found them."

"Another possible reason," Ralph suggested, "is that Carrington could have been taking his diamonds direct to London, where he'd get better prices from the cutters for his parcel of stones." He grinned. "Just a thought."

"And thank you for it, Ralph," Leroy said. He leaned back in his seat and relaxed, filled with a pleasant sense of accomplishment. "Q.E.D."

"Not quite," Danforth disagreed. "One thing still needs explaining. After Carrington accumulated his store of diamonds at the river's mouth, where did he conceal them for the trip back to Johannesburg with you, Ralph? Must have been quite a bundle to hide."

"Not in the car," Ralph said positively. "We unloaded the boot every evening—even took out the car seats to sit on. I handled all the equipment every day—rod cases, tackle box, food supplies, everything. Nothing concealed."

"How about a money belt?"

Ralph shook his head. "No money belt. And not in his pockets. He only wore shorts and a shirt."

"Well, confound it, think!" Danforth said with pretended impatience. "They must have been somewhere."

Ralph steered expertly around a sharp bend. "If you'll forgive me, Mr. Danforth," he said with an apologetic expression, "I don't think there were any diamonds. Mr. Carrington took a fishing trip, and he found he'd inherited a fortune when we returned to Joburg. That's all."

Danforth laughed. "Didn't you notice anything out of the ordinary on your return trip to Johannesburg?"

"Not a single thing. Unless you'd call a fresh hole in Mr. Carrington's mosquito net out of the ordinary?"

Danforth sat erect. "Very suspicious. How'd that happen?"

"He burned it with a cigarette."

"Did you see him do it?"

"No. He told me afterward."

"How big a hole?"

"Six inches across, I suppose."

"Was it charred at the edges as though from burning?"

"I don't remember."

"So," said Leroy who had been thinking as he listened. "The whole thing explains itself. Did you run out of gas anywhere on the way home, Ralph?"

"Yes. Once."

"And did Carrington pour your spare gasoline into the tank from your emergency can?"

"Yes, he did. I was getting some water out of a stream nearby to fill the radiator."

"That does it," Leroy said. "It's quite simple, really. Carrington hid his diamonds in your spare can of gasoline, Ralph. And when, unexpectedly, you had to use the spare gasoline, he cut a piece out of his mosquito netting to serve as a strainer over the spout of the can—so the diamonds he'd hidden in it wouldn't tumble into your gas tank along with the spare gas. How's that for an idea?"

Ralph looked at him with admiration. "My word, Mr. Leroy," he said, "you do have an imagination, don't you?"

* * * *

They stopped at the Hottentot Kop Hotel for dinner and the night. Perched on a high bluff, the hotel overlooked a magnificent panorama of green hills, fertile valleys, and distant mountains capped with the violet mist of approaching evening.

They ordered a lavish dinner, deliberately chosen by Carol and Helen in defiance of its caloric content; they drank a bottle of velvety South African wine with the meal and were very gay, the men proposing several toasts to their brilliant solution of what they decided to call The African Fish Mystery. And they were smoking a postprandial cigarette on the verandah, watching the darkening view, when Ralph Muir came running up the verandah steps and joined them.

His usually calm demeanor was illumined by an almost incandescent excitement. At their invitation he sat down between Helen and Carol and said in a voice he strove to make calm, "I've been working on the car. Wanted to correct that engine sputter before starting out tomorrow."

Helen said, "Did you find the trouble?"

"I found it, Mrs. Leroy." His words were tense. "It wasn't in the plugs, or carburetor or feed lines. It was in the petrol tank itself. Look!"

He held out a clenched hand, liberally blackened with grease, and opened it before their eyes.

"Pebbles," said Carol. "How peculiar." Suddenly her eyes widened.

"Not pebbles," Ralph announced. "Diamonds!" He gulped. "They were in my petrol tank! When one of them would shift on a rough bit of road over to the tank outlet, it blocked the flow of petrol for a moment and we'd get that engine sputter!"

They stared, fascinated, at the five rough diamonds in his hand. None was more than an inch in diameter.

King Danforth clicked his tongue deprecatingly. "We missed that," he told his partner gently. "It seems that Duke Carrington actually poured a few diamonds into Ralph's tank before he thought to use the mosquito net strainer!"

Leroy reached out and patted Ralph on top of the head. "You're rich, Ralph," he said. "Congratulations."

Ralph began to stutter something. But Danforth and Leroy weren't listening.

They were smiling at each other over their wives' heads with the pride and mutual respect of two small boys who have climbed unscathed to the topmost limb of the tallest tree in the orchard.

The Italian Tile Mystery

It was raining in Positano. The rain bounced off the red-tile roofs, spattered in the gutters of the golden cathedral dome, turned the steep narrow streets into sluiceways. And with the onslaught of the rain all the quaint sunshiny charm that endeared this cliffside village to tourists immediately deserted it, leaving behind an atmosphere of wintry cheerlessness. The pervasive dampness penetrated not only the public rooms of the Savoia Hotel but the very bones of the hotel's guests.

Martin and Helen Leroy sat with King and Carol Danforth in wing chairs before a tiny fire in the lounge. Bundled in bulky sweaters and sports jackets, they stared bleakly through the rain-stippled window to the sullenly breathing Mediterranean below.

"We should have stayed on the Valhalla," Helen said, "where it was warm."

"Or the bar of the Excelsior Hotel in Naples," her husband said wistfully. "There's the place to spend a rainy afternoon."

Yet it was this very rain that led Danforth and Leroy into one of the most challenging mysteries they encountered during their cruise around the world on the ship *Valhalla*, now tied up in Naples just a few miles away. The two mystery-story writers (known to their legion of fans by their collaboration team-name of "Leroy King") especially relished the Positano affair because it made more stringent demands on their ingenuity than had even the notable adventure of the African Fish Mystery.

The old-fashioned clock on the wall whirred, preparatory to striking four. Mrs. Cardoni, who owned and managed the small hotel, bustled into the room. She held a large tray before her like an offering. "Tea," she announced cheerfully. "Hot tea. Good for rainy afternoons and depressed people."

They welcomed her. They would have welcomed anything at that point except more rain. "Where will you have it?" Mrs. Cardoni asked.

"Right here in front of the fire,"

Helen suggested. "Is there a table?"

Her hands being occupied, Mrs. Cardoni pointed with her chin. "There," she said, "by the window."

Leroy rose and went to the window. He lifted a low, tile-topped coffee table and brought it over before the fire. "Just the ticket," he said. "Gather round, people. Put down the free lunch, Mrs. Cardoni, and we'll pitch in. Join us?"

Mrs. Cardoni was pleased. "I hoped you'd ask me," she said. "I brought an extra cup."

Carol Danforth said warmly, "Pour for us, Mrs. Cardoni, please." They liked their landlady very much. She was a plump, amiable widow with a heart as big as her impressive bosom. She treated them, mere guests in her hotel, like members of her own family.

After tea Mrs. Cardoni removed the tray and Carol Danforth sighed. "Still raining," she said lugubriously. Her eyes passed lightly across the table before her. "My word!" she said. "Look at the table you brought us, Martin."

"What about it?" Leroy asked.

"Take your feet off it for a minute, King," Helen directed, "so we can see all of it."

Danforth complied.

"Just a tile table, darling," Helen said after giving it a brief glance. "Rather interesting tiles, I'll admit, and quite attractive."

Danforth lit a cigarette. "Charming," he said lazily.

Carol raised a hand to her short dark hair. "I've never seen a more peculiar collection of tiles in my life," she said with more animation than she had exhibited all day.

For the first time, all four really focused their attention

on the low coffee table before them. Its top consisted of four rows of tiles, four tiles to a row—sixteen tiles in all—surrounded by a molding of painted wood. Each tile was about six inches wide by nine inches deep, so that the full table top was approximately twenty-four inches by thirty-six inches—two by three feet.

The background color of all the tiles was white and each tile contained a scene or an object obviously hand-painted on the clay before the tile had been given its final ceramic glaze in the kiln.

There was nothing unusual about the construction of the table or its overall decorative effect. Indeed, the white backgrounds of the tiles gave the table top a simple harmonious unity. But when one examined the scenes depicted on the individual tiles, one saw what Carol Danforth meant when she called them a "peculiar collection."

For the pictures seemed to bear no relationship to each other whatsoever. One was of a mountain top; another of a large figure 7 with olive leaves floating across it; a third showed a staff of music; a fourth, a wall with a hole in it. Viewed separately, the sixteen tiles formed a mélange of subjects and colors that might well have been the product of a demented mind.

Danforth stretched his lanky figure in his chair. "This table top could set the tile industry back a thousand years," he remarked.

"It isn't that bad," Leroy protested. The dark eyes in his Indian-like face flashed. "It's an unholy mess in an artistic sense, but it looks pretty attractive at that, just as Helen says."

"Like a wife after you've been married for a while," said Helen with a side glance at her husband. "Usually a mess, but occasionally quite attractive." Helen was blonde, statuesque, and lovely. She grinned impishly.

"You're fishing for compliments again," Leroy said. "I wonder who made this table top? It must be unique. There can't be two like it in the whole world."

Mrs. Cardoni passed through the lounge on her way to check on the dinner. Danforth hailed her. "Mrs. Cardoni, we're admiring your beautiful tile table. Where did it come from, if I'm not being impertinent? Is it Italian?"

"In a way," Mrs. Cardoni said, smiling. "It was made right here in Positano especially for me—but by an American gentleman."

Helen said, "We thought some of the pictures on the tiles seemed a little...well, odd."

The landlady flapped her apron with the air of a woman who is about to enjoy a good gossip. "I'll tell you about that table," she said, resting one hip on a chair arm. "One of my guests in the hotel made it. He had a permanent room here for several years until he became ill and died. He was an American like you, but he lived in Italy almost all his life."

"What was his name?" Carol asked. She had a passion for names.

"Lemuel V. Bishop," Mrs. Cardoni replied. She paused a moment, her eyes blank with memory. "His only relative was a brother—a famous lawyer in America, he told me, who did not approve of him because he was an impractical, absent-minded professor who loved Italy more than the United States. He was a lonely man while he lived here at the hotel. He didn't make friends with anybody else, not even the other guests. He'd been a teacher in Ravenna, he said, and now he was old and tired and wished to spend the rest of his life in Positano, where he could see the sea and the golden dome of the cathedral and the fishing boats overturned on the black beach."

They listened sympathetically. "But what about the table?" Leroy prodded gently.

"Oh, yes, the table. After Mr. Bishop became seriously ill, he began to make the table. He got clay and paints and all the materials to make the table itself in the village. And he amused himself for several months up in his room, cutting the tiles and painting them, and putting the table together. He got Giovanni Polito, our local tile maker, to fire his tiles after he'd painted the designs on them."

"But you said he made them for you," Carol said, scenting a faded romance.

"He did. But just as a personal gift for me, because he thought I'd been kind to him while he was sick."

"No wonder he wanted to show his appreciation," Leroy murmured. "It is a handsome table."

"I think so, too," she said, "although Mr. Bishop always made a joke about it."

"A joke?" asked Danforth curiously.

"Sometimes I'd go into his room when he was working on his tiles and he'd laugh and say this would be one will his stuffy brother might have trouble reading."

Danforth and Leroy exchanged glances. "You say he called the table a will?" King asked.

"Yes. In a joking way. He told me it was his last will and testament, and he was going to leave it with me. And when he died, his brother in America would come and get it." Mrs. Cardoni paused. "He was, of course, joking. No brother ever came."

"How would the brother know he was dead?"

"Mr. Bishop said he wrote his brother a letter several weeks before the end," she explained, "and told him he was dying and that I had his will. And he asked his brother to come here and handle things for him. He also said he told his brother in the letter that he wanted to be buried in Italy—in Ravenna."

"But no brother came."

"No."

"Are you sure he mailed the letter?"

"I mailed it for him myself—airmail. That's when he told me what was in it."

"What did you do when no brother showed up?"

"I used what money he had left to bury him in Ravenna

as he asked."

They regarded her in silence for a moment. This was a service above and beyond the call of duty from a hotelkeeper to a guest. Mrs. Cardoni smiled and said. "Mr. Bishop was a fine man. So kind and scholarly and gentle. And a very good guest. He stayed here many months and never complained once about anything. And he always paid his bills promptly."

"Thanks, Mrs. Cardoni," Helen said. "We didn't intend to remind you of what must have been a painful incident. We're sorry."

The *albergatore* waved a hand and rose. "There are all kinds of problems in our trade," she said. "One does one's best." She disappeared into the kitchen.

Carol frowned at her husband and said, "All right, now, darling, I can see the wheels going around in that inquisitive head of yours."

"Why not?" Leroy said. "This could come right out of one of our books, King. A dying man, a will, a stuffy attorney, a kindly innkeeper. Am I right?"

"Completely," his partner said with enthusiasm. "I'll bet Mr. Lemuel V. Bishop wasn't kidding. These screwy pictures on the tiles must mean something."

Carol burst out, "But that's ridiculous! It couldn't be. Or the brother would have arrived to take charge after Mr. Bishop died."

"Ah, my sweet," said Danforth, smiling, "that is exactly where one of my meager talents confirms my guess that there's something to this odd business."

"You mean you've got talent?" his wife asked with a laugh. "I prefer money, darling."

"I just happen," returned Danforth with dignity, "to have total recall when it comes to news stories, as you very well know. And I distinctly remember that a New York attorney named Clyde R. Bishop was killed two years ago when that big Italian airliner crashed on take-off from Idlewild."

Carol said, "If you remember it, it happened." She turned to Helen. "You see? It's like being married to a computing machine."

Leroy said, "Are you serious, King?"

"Certainly I'm serious. A New York lawyer named Bishop was listed among the fatalities in that crash. See what I'm getting at?"

"That lawyer—Bishop may have been flying here, in response to his dying brother's letter when his plane cracked up and he was killed?"

"Doesn't it fit?"

"Like a suede glove by Barra!" said Leroy enthusiastically.

"And that's why nobody came to read this will?" Helen said, touching the tile table with the point of one dainty shoe.

"Exactly," her husband said. "And that means it probably is a will. And all these months it's just been sitting here in this lounge waiting for someone as brilliant as 'Leroy King' to come along and figure it out, and see that Mr. Bishop's heirs come into their rightful inheritance. Doesn't that sound completely reasonable?"

"It sounds suspiciously like boasting to me," Carol remarked. "But what are we waiting for? Let's get started. I was always a whiz at crossword puzzles."

"Me too," Helen chimed in, "especially on the really tough words like gnu and poi and pyx." She flashed her wonderful smile. "This little old table top shouldn't take us more than a few minutes."

"What we need," said Danforth, "is a system. If the tiles really mean something, we ought to go at the problem scientifically. Don't you think so, Mart?"

"I do. It seems obvious that the tiles must represent words or groups of words. So let's try the simplest system first. Let's write down the words we can think of that best describe each tile."

Helen said, "Shall I be secretary?"

"Please do," said King Danforth gallantly. "I can't imagine a lovelier amanuensis."

"Hey!" Carol interjected. "Why don't you ever say nice things like that to me?"

"You're my wife. And dignified restraint is therefore indicated in my remarks to you." He grinned at his wife and added softly, "At least in public."

Carol flushed. "Come on," she said, "quit stalling. We have work to do "

Leroy said to Helen, "Make a rough sketch of the table top, honey. And number the tiles from one to sixteen. Then identify each tile as we describe it to you. Okay? Tile Number One: a signpost with a hand-shaped sign pointing west. Got it?"

"Got it," Helen said, busily writing. And when Leroy and Danforth had finished describing each tile, her notes looked like this:

1. Hand-shaped sign pointing west
2. Colonial building with sign "The Anchor"
3. Mountain scene
4. Sky and clouds
5. Woman looking at basket on doorstep
6. House on hillside
7. Wall with hole in it
8. Seascape
9. Oil lamp burning
10. Tea cup being emptied
11. Man buckling sword belt
12. Figure 7 with leaves
13. Baby waving
14. Man singing, holding open book
15. Building with egg-crate type walls
16. 8-note scale on musical stall

The Italian Tile Mystery | 51

"Now," said Leroy, "everybody look at tile Number One. And say, in turn, the word or words you think accurately describes the picture on it. This is a bona fide brainstorm session, now. We don't want anybody criticizing anybody else's suggestions till we've got them all down. Okay?"

"Okay," said the others in chorus.

"Good. Then you start, Carol."

They looked hard at tile Number One. "Sign," said Carol.

"West," said Danforth.

"Pointing," Helen suggested.

"Left," was Leroy's guess.

Helen wrote the four words down under the proper tile number.

Carol said, "That one sounded like sign language."

They ignored her. "Second tile," Danforth said. "Colonial building with a sign reading 'The Anchor'."

"Inn," said Carol promptly. "Pub."

"Hotel."

"Seamen's rest."

They began to enjoy themselves. Helen wrote the words as they were uttered and before very long Helen's word list looked like this:

1. sign west pointing left
2. inn pub hotel seaman's rest
3. peak hill crag mountain
4. sky firmament cloud 9 heaven
5. Foundling deserted marketing good Samaritan
6. cliff home Savoia hotel
7. Humpty-Dumpty peek-a-boo aperture opening
8. ocean waves main sea
9. lamp light glow quick
10. grounds dregs good-to-last-drop lees
11. knight sword belt gird
12. Seven Seven Seven Leaves
13. Cheerio bye-bye so long see you later
14. song music singing hymn
15. Hilton school factory hotel
16. octave scale staff do-re-mi

They passed the completed list from hand to hand, studying it, switching their eyes like shuttlecocks back and forth between the listed words and the tiles on the table top.

"Now what?" asked Carol.

"Now," her husband said, "we begin to eliminate. We bring to bear the cool, critical judgment which Leroy King himself displays at all times in his novels. We select the one word for each tile that seems to make the most sense when combined with the others."

"Wait." Leroy was staring at the list. "Maybe we can find a hook to hang our decoding on, if we can figure out why three of these tiles are so similar."

"What's that mean?" Helen asked. "I don't see any tiles that look alike."

"Look at Numbers Two, Six, and Fifteen," Leroy said.

"Bingo!" Danforth said suddenly. "I get it. All three are buildings, and in all three cases one of us suggested the same word to describe them—the word 'hotel.' Right?"

"Right. And Helen even said 'Savoia' to describe tile Number Six—the very hotel in which we are sitting at this moment."

"Sure. But I doubt if the word we want for all three of those tiles is 'hotel.' The sentence in the tiles is probably too short to use 'hotel' in it three times with any significance."

"How about 'inn,' then?" Danforth asked. "Spelled with one 'n' it's a very common word and might easily be used three times in a short sentence."

"Let's try it. Write down the word 'in' opposite tile Numbers Two, Six, and Fifteen, Helen." Helen followed instructions. "That's the only similarity I can see," Danforth proceeded. "So we'll have to assume that each of the other tiles represents a separate word. In which case, what might the first word be, tile Number One, that would make sense coming before the word 'in'?"

Helen looked at her list. "I favor the word 'left' for tile Number One," she said thoughtfully. "It sounds like a word that would be used in a will, don't you think?"

"Not having been left anything by rich relatives, I couldn't say," Leroy grinned. "But if that's your woman's intuition, I'll buy it. First two words, therefore, are 'Left in'."

"We're doing famously," said Danforth. "We're already one-eighth finished."

"I see no reason to bat our brains out on the next two

tiles," Leroy said. "In each case only one of the suggested words honestly describes the tiles. So let's put down our first row of tiles to mean: 'Left in mountain sky'."

Helen sucked on her lower lip and looked stubborn. "That's silly," she protested. " 'Left in mountain sky'! Is this a new kind of air-conditioned safe deposit vault Mr. Bishop is directing us to?"

"It does seem rather meaningless," Leroy admitted.

At this point Danforth began to display the signs that always portended an announcement of immense importance from him. He cleared his throat, rubbed a hand over his crew-cut briskly, and said, "I think we should all have a drink."

There was no objection to this eminently sensible deduction, so they ordered vodka gimlets all around from Guiseppi, the bartender-waiter of the hotel, who brought the cocktails to them on a classic silver tray that could have come from the ruins of Paestum.

"Now," said Danforth when the first sip of the gimlets had won unanimous approval, "may I parade a little of the perspicacity and analytical skill that, combined with Martin Leroy's, have made us famous?"

"By all means," his wife encouraged. "You look like the cat that has swallowed the cream."

"I must warn you against mixing metaphors, baby," Danforth said. "But no matter. Look at the words we have put down after tiles Four and Twelve. Notice anything about them?"

Silence. Intensive study of the indicated words. Nothing. Leroy said, "Give."

"Gladly," Danforth said grandiloquently. "I shall read them aloud and then, perhaps, the light—"

"Hold it!" Helen exclaimed. "They rhyme! Look, 'heaven' in the first batch and 'seven' in the other! 'Heaven, seven'."

"Head of the class," King said. "Now take a look at the words for tiles Eight and Sixteen."

Leroy shook his head. " 'Sea' rhymes with 'do-re-mi,' I suppose. But 'do-re-mi' seems an unlikely word to end a sentence. That's the last word, remember."

"Look at the tile again," Danforth said. "All the notes on the staff are quarter notes except the third one. It's a half note. And it's 'mi.' So what about Mr. Bishop just wanting the 'mi' to be used? Spelled with an 'e'?"

Leroy nodded. "Let's try it. 'Me', for the last word, Helen."

Helen wrote it down.

"Now," said Leroy, "if we use the words that rhyme for the end tiles, our first line would read: 'Left in mountain heaven.'"

"And the rest of the message comes out like this," Danforth said. "Left in mountain heaven Blank in blank sea Blank blank blank seven Blank blank in me."

"Clear as mud," Helen laughed. "All we have to do is fill in the blanks and somebody will inherit a tile-topped table."

Leroy was staring at the table top. "If it rhymes, maybe it's a short poem. And if it's a poem, it ought to scan."

"Modern poetry," Carol suggested, "doesn't scan once in a hundred times. That's effete and old-fashioned, didn't you know?"

"I refuse to acknowledge, even remotely, that Mr. Bishop might have been writing modern verse in tiles!" her husband reproved her. "He was a classicist, I'm sure. A teacher in Ravenna. So let's say, for the heck of it, that he intended his tile poem to scan. Where does that get us?"

"In deep trouble," Leroy said. "None of the words we thought of for tile Number Five is monosyllabic. And it would have to be—to scan like the first row of tiles."

"Suppose we use part of that first word under tile Number Five?" Carol said tentatively. "'Foundling' is obviously an accurate description of the picture. But just 'found' could describe it, too. A baby in a basket being 'found'—

get it?"

"Sounds good," her husband said. "I only hope that doesn't mean Mr. Bishop was leaving a foundling to somebody in his will. That way lies madness. However, if we use 'found,' the second row of tiles reads: 'Found in opening sea.'"

"Wait, though, darling," Carol protested. "How come you used 'opening' for that third word?"

"It scans."

"And besides," Helen chimed in, "it would be silly to talk about a humpty-dumpty sea or a peek-a-boo sea or an aperture sea."

"This whole thing is nuts anyway," Carol said. "And there's something quite appealing to me about the phrase 'humpty-dumpty sea.' It speaks to me somehow. But I'll bow to the will of the majority—'opening' it is. So we've got: "Left in mountain heaven Found in opening sea Quick blank blank seven—"

"Just a minute, Carol," King Danforth interrupted. "You said 'quick' for the first word in the third row of tiles. Why quick? The tile shows an oil lamp."

"I see why." Helen patted Carol's hand. "You're just a genius, darling, that's all. Certainly it's 'quick.' There's the wick in the lamp. And look at the odd shape of the lamp handle—that little handle-loop coming off to the right, it's shaped exactly like a Q. So 'Q' plus 'wick' spells 'quick'."

"I concede defeat," said Danforth with mock humility. "I guess you are pretty good at crossword puzzles at that."

"How about that next tile, though?" Leroy asked. "The teacup being emptied? Three of our descriptive words would scan there. We could have 'quick grounds,' 'quick dregs' or 'quick lees'." Helen laughed. "Quick grounds seems to go more with coffee or divorce," she said, "than with a will."

Leroy was silent for an instant, holding up his hand dramatically. "Man," he said finally, "I think I've got hold of one from way out. Look. If the second tile in that row is 'lees' it makes a faintly familiar word when combined with the word ahead of it, 'quick.' The two together would read "quick lees'."

"An adverb if I ever heard one," said Carol. "But spelled wrong. Shouldn't have an 's' on the end."

"And it's never used any more in the singular," Danforth added, "that word 'lees'."

"Let me finish. What if the final 's' is a possessive? Then what do we get?"

"Something that belongs to quickly, whoever that is."

"Shakespeare!" Danforth cried. "Mistress Quickly! Merry Wives of Windsor!"

"Who else?" Leroy said smugly. "Who else ever had a name like that?"

"But why Mistress Quickly?" Helen argued. "What's she got to do with tile tables or Mr. Bishop's will?"

"Mistress Quickly," said Leroy, "if I remember correctly, was a servant to Doctor Caius in Shakespeare's play. She waited on him, served as his messenger, did his housekeeping, played hostess for him—"

"Ah!" Danforth nodded approvingly. "In a word, she was a kind of Mrs. Cardoni ? Because Mrs. Cardoni served in the same capacity for Mr. Bishop so faithfully? You think that Quickly in this rebus refers to Mrs. Cardoni?"

"Indubitably," said Leroy. "What do you think, girls?" They were staring at him with doubt plain on their faces.

"Well," said Helen with a kind of reluctant admiration, "you certainly reached for that one, darling. I suppose it could be."

"The verse ought to be easy from here on," Leroy proclaimed. "Which of the four words describing the next tile, Number Eleven, could belong to Mrs. Cardoni? 'Knight'—'sword'—'belt'—'gird'?"

"Ouch!" Helen said.

"Personally," said Danforth, "I find all of them slightly ludicrous when applied to our excellent landlady. Cardoni's knight? Not likely, however you spell 'knight.' Cardoni's sword? Huh-uh. Cardoni's belt? Well..."

"But how about the next one, King?" Carol asked. "Cardoni's 'gird.' Couldn't that be girdle?"

"Please!" said Leroy. "Mrs. Cardoni is amply favored above the waist, but her hips and waist line are quite trim. Girdle? It's unthinkable!"

"Hold it!" It was Danforth's turn to strike the pose of The Thinker. "I direct your attention to the tile itself. What is the man doing in the picture?"

"Putting on his sword."

"Yes. Now what's another way of saying 'put on' when one refers to a sword?"

"Arm," said Leroy. "Buckle on, clip on, gird on..."

"Gird on," Danforth said, pleased. "Just the word. Gird on. Guerdon."

The girls regarded him blankly. "Are you sure that gimlet hasn't been too much for you?" Helen asked solicitously. "What's a 'guerdon'?—if I may exhibit my stupidity."

"A guerdon is a word less common now than formerly. But it means a reward."

"Oh!" Carol's lips moved as she read over to herself the message of the tiles with the new word added. "So the third row of tiles reads: 'Quickly's guerdon seven'," she said aloud. "Seven what?"

Helen consulted her notes. "Seven 'cheerio, bye-bye, so long, or see you later.' I've heard of saying good bye several times, but seven farewells seems excessive."

"Tile Number Twelve is the only one with any leaves in it," Leroy said. "Those lovely, curving olive leaves are floating across the big figure Seven in the picture. Maybe Bishop wants us to notice the leaves."

"So—seven leaves. What's that mean?"

"Perhaps the rest of the tiles will tell us."

"All right. The first tile in the last row, Number Thirteen: a baby waving. 'Bye-bye' seems the logical choice."

"Or just 'by'," Helen suggested.

"Next," intoned Danforth, "we come to the final word—the one that rounds out this cryptic message. And it better be good. Because so far the whole thing makes as little sense as a series of undeciphered hieroglyphics."

"Maybe this last word will prove a Rosetta Stone," said Leroy smiling. "What's your fancy, ladies and gentleman? 'Seven leaves by song in me'? 'Seven leaves by music in me'? 'Seven leaves by hymn in me'? Or 'seven leaves by singing in me'?"

They all preferred 'hymn,' spelled 'him' since it was the only word that even approached intelligibility in its context.

"Now read the whole thing. Helen," Leroy directed.

> "Left in mountain heaven
> Found in opening sea
> Quickly's guerdon seven
> Leaves by him in me."

For a moment they were silent. Then Danforth sighed and shrugged and said gloomily, "Let's eat. It was a pleasant way to pass the time on a rainy afternoon. That's all I can say for it."

They went into the dining room. Helen, leading the way, was heard to murmur to Carol, "If our table in the dining room has a tile top, I'll scream!"

During the meal they chattered about everything but Mrs. Cardoni's tile coffee table. Nevertheless, from their preoccupied manner, Danforth and Leroy continued to think about it. When dinner was over, they moved into the lounge again for coffee. Mrs. Cardoni served it to them on Mr. Bishop's table.

"Listen," said Leroy when they were alone once more. "I hate to give up on this table rebus, don't you, King? It's a gorgeous puzzle."

"Who's giving up?" his partner said stoutly. "I needed to renew my strength with a few vitamins, that's all. I've been thinking. What about Bishop's background? We may find a clue there. What did he do in Ravenna? Teach?"

"Yes."

"All right." Danforth rubbed his cropped head. "What did he teach ?"

"I'll find out." Leroy got up and went out into the small lobby of the hotel. Mrs. Cardoni was behind the desk, entering figures in a ledger. He said, "What was Mr. Bishop's specialty as a teacher in Ravenna, Mrs. Cardoni? Do you happen to know?"

"Of course," she replied. "Mr. Bishop was an authority on Italian literature."

"Thanks. That might prove helpful."

"Are you still trying to make sense out of those tiles?" she asked. "I'm really afraid you're wasting your time. The table is merely Mr. Bishop's legacy to me. It's all he had except the money I used to bury him with."

"You're probably right," Leroy said. He went back to the lounge and reported.

"Italian literature!" Danforth said, beaming. "That opens up a whole new field! Bishop ran to literary allusions apparently, judging from the Mistress Quickly bit. So maybe Italian literature holds the key."

"If there's any literature in the world I know nothing about," Carol said, "it's Italian. Let's play bridge."

Helen said, "I've read Dante's *Inferno*."

For an instant an electric silence held Danforth and Leroy. Then they began to speak simultaneously. Both stopped short. Then they grinned at each other—the familiar partnership grin they usually reserved for use when one of their complicated mystery plots had at last come right.

"Dante!" said Leroy.

"Dante!" echoed Danforth happily-

"Did I say something bright?" Helen asked. "If so, please

explain it to me."

Martin Leroy said, "This may be the key, baby. You said you'd read Dante's *Inferno*. Have you ever read the entire *Divine Comedy*?"

"Not me. *Inferno* was more than enough for me, thank you."

Her husband went on. "The other two parts of the Divine Comedy are *Purgatory* and *Paradise*, and that's interesting, because the first line of tiles refers to 'heaven'—or paradise, if you prefer."

Danforth broke in. "Mart! Didn't Mrs. Cardoni say Bishop's name was Lemuel V. Bishop?"

"Yes?"

"Then the middle initial 'V' may be significant."

Leroy nodded. "Virgil!" he said. Their wives looked at them as though they had taken leave of their senses. "Virgil!" said Helen. "I thought it was Dante."

"Don't you remember?" her husband asked blandly. "It was Virgil who guided Dante through Hell in the *Inferno*."

"Oh!"

Danforth said, " 'Left in mountain heaven'—our first row of tiles. That means Virgil left Dante when they got to Paradise which was located at the top of the mountain of Purgatory, as I recall it. Because when they reached Paradise, the lovely Beatrice took over the guiding job from Virgil."

"And the second row of tiles!" Leroy almost shouted. "'Found in opening sea.' I'll give you three to one the 'sea' at the end of the row is supposed to be the letter 'C' and not an ocean. Get it?"

"Don't ask me," Carol said, "I never even read the *Inferno!*"

"It must stand for 'Canto'," Leroy said. "Virgil found Dante in the first part of the poem. In the opening Canto, as our verse says."

"So Virgil left Dante in heaven and found him in the first verse of the *Inferno*," Helen said. "Why should Bishop tell us that? That doesn't sound like part of a will."

"For identification purposes," Danforth said slowly. "To point to Dante as the 'him' of the tile verse. And to serve as a kind of signature to his will by calling attention to Virgil—if his middle name was really Virgil."

"It was," said Mrs. Cardoni, who had quietly come into the room behind them. She stood with her mouth slightly open, listening, her magnificent bosom visibly swelling and collapsing as she breathed.

"Okay," Leroy said. "Next: 'Quickly's reward seven'." Maddeningly, he broke off to grin at Mrs. Cardoni and interpolate, "That's you, Mrs. Cardoni. He calls you Mistress Quickly here in the tiles."

She merely stared at him.

"Quickly's guerdon seven," Danforth said. "Punctuate that properly and it makes more sense. Simply put a colon after 'guerdon'."

"Right. 'Quickly's guerdon—or reward: seven leaves by him in me."

They all saw it at once.

"Leaves—pages!" Leroy cried.

"By Dante!" Helen said in awe.

"In me," Danforth finished, his tone expressing infinite satisfaction. "That must be the table. 'In me'. Not in Virgil, obviously. In the tile-topped table itself."

Mrs. Cardoni drew closer and stared with new fascination at the colorful tiles of the table top. "What does it mean, Mr. Leroy?" she asked in bewilderment.

"If it means what I think it means, you're going to inherit something pretty valuable."

"Valuable!" Danforth said. "Priceless is the word. Do you know something, my illiterate friends? Not a single manuscript page, not a line of handwriting, not one signature of Dante's has survived to our time. There just ain't any. So even if this should prove to be just seven printed pages of an early edition of great Dante's works, it will be priceless.

And if it's actually part of the manuscript of the *Divine Comedy*..."

Carol interrupted him. "Wait now, darling," she said earnestly. "Don't get Mrs. Cardoni's hopes up and then dash them. It's not fair. This whole thing is quite probably silly, Mrs. Cardoni. We've built up a message in the tiles from a crazy-quilt of words we selected quite arbitrarily, and then we've interpreted that message on the basis of clues so fragile as to be almost non-existent. You can see our chances of being right are just about a thousand to one."

"It is pretty far-fetched," her husband admitted. "But I honestly think we might—"

Carol interrupted him a second time. "All right. But why, if there is anything hidden under the tiles of the table, would Mr. Bishop have put it there in the first place, going to all this tile-painting and tablemaking trouble? Why not just hand it to Mrs. Cardoni and say, 'Here are some pages of Dante manuscript I want you to have when I die.'"

Leroy nodded. "A fair question, Carol. I think there may have been several reasons. First, I'm sure he must have been needling his lawyer brother just a bit in his quiet, scholarly way. He wanted to give this practical, serious-minded attorney a brand-new kind of will to decipher and file for probate! No doubt he gave his brother some cryptic clue to the reading of the tiles in his letter, so there would be no chance the message would not be read; but can you imagine his brother's embarrassment, carting this tile-topped table into the office of the register of wills or whatever it is, and trying to file it? Remember, Lemuel V. Bishop was presumably steeped in the literature and history of Italy, and to present his stuffy brother with a challenge of such Renaissance deviousness must have amused him."

"I must say it has delighted you," Carol smiled.

"The chief reason he did it," Danforth suggested, "was probably to protect Mrs. Cardoni's interests. Whatever's in the table, if it has anything to do with Dante, must be priceless, as I say. And Bishop didn't want Mrs. Cardoni, a babe in the woods in such a matter, to be cheated of her legacy's proper value if she should try to dispose of it herself. Bishop wanted his brother to handle it for her, so she'd be sure to get her rights."

Helen said, "You make it sound kind of convincing. But where, I can't help wondering, could Mr. Bishop have found anything like a Dante manuscript to begin with?'

"In Ravenna, probably," Danforth hazarded. "Dante was a political exile from Florence, his hometown, for a long time, you know. He died in Ravenna, I believe. So maybe Bishop had been rooting through dusty archives there most of his life, searching through old trunks in people's attics, and came across this treasure, whatever it is. Anyway, will you girls please stop with the questions and let us take this table apart? I am not a patient man, and Mrs. Cardoni is politely trying to keep from bursting with curiosity at this very moment." He smiled at the landlady who was indeed trembling with excitement. "Are you willing to let us commit mayhem on your table, Mrs. Cardoni ?"

"For such a purpose, how can I refuse?"

"Good." Danforth turned the coffee table over so that its tiled top rested on the rug and its four legs pointed toward the ceiling. The legs were screwed on individually. And there was no sign of any other screwhead on the plywood undersurface of the table. "We may have to break the tiles to get at those seven leaves," he said regretfully.

Leroy said, "Let's take the legs off first. Do you have a screwdriver handy, Mrs. Cardoni?"

She secured one from the hotel pantry in record time.

Leroy loosened the screws that held the table's tapered legs in place and removed them. Once the legs were off, four more screwheads appeared, one in each corner where the base of the leg had hidden it.

Helen, Carol, and Mrs. Cardoni leaned breathlessly over

his shoulder as Leroy loosened these screws in turn. When the last screw came free, he inserted the tip of the screwdriver along the edge of the plywood and pried gently. The whole square of plywood came readily away.

They stared down at what lay between this false bottom, just removed, and the wooden base on which the tiles had been set.

Seven sheets of heavy, parchment-like vellum, yellowed with age and covered with spidery handwriting in faded brownish ink, stared back at them. Each sheet had been sealed by Lemuel V. Bishop into a transparent, damp-proof envelope of cellophane.

Mrs. Cardoni took a corset-creaking breath, speechless with astonishment. Impulsively, Carol put her arms around the landlady and hugged her. Leroy muttered, "Seven leaves, by Jove!"

But Danforth said in a disappointed, puzzled voice, "But that's Latin, not Italian vernacular! It can't be part of the Divine Comedy manuscript!"

He leaned down over Leroy's shoulder and delicately, with his fingertips, moved aside several of the sheets that overlapped others, revealing the lower portion of sheet Number Seven—the one that had been hidden underneath. "Look!" he breathed. "Latin, Italian, or Sanskrit—what's the difference? Do you see what that is?"

They followed his pointing finger with their eyes. They saw the two words, unmistakably clear and unblurred even through the cellophane, and written in the same spidery script as the rest: Dante Alighieri.

"His signature!" Danforth said. "As sure as his own Hell!" He looked up into Mrs. Cardoni's face. "Mrs. Cardoni," he said solemnly, "if that is an authentic signature, you can change your name to Mrs. Croesus."

* * * *

The *Valhalla* left Naples the following afternoon for Piraeus. The Danforths and Leroys were aboard to continue their cruise around the world. They had personally committed Mrs. Cardoni and her seven "leaves" to the scholarly ministrations of the Director of the Naples Biblioteca, a man named Pietro Carlo who providentially turned out to be distantly related to her dead husband's family. He had promised faithfully to look after Mrs. Cardoni's interests in the matter of the manuscript pages as well as to advise them just what her legacy consisted of when he should have settled that controversial question.

But it was not until the unbelievable beauty of Greece lay behind them and the *Valhalla* was making for Port Said and the Suez Canal at a steady twenty knots that they heard the final word on their Positano adventure.

They were having dinner when a steward brought Danforth a radiogram. He tore it open. "It's from Carlo, in Naples," he said, and proceeded to read its contents aloud:

"Happy to report your find seems authentic. Evidently fragment of rough draft of letter written in Latin by Dante to his most illustrious protector while in exile, Can Grande della Scala of Verona, immortalized in 17th Canto of Paradisio. Letter is famous, containing directions for interpreting *Divina Commedia*. This rough draft conforms in most respects with accepted text of that letter, of which original mss., along with all other Dante mss., has been lost. Signature alone worth millions. But Mrs. Cardoni has agreed to make a gift of legacy to Italy, provided it be officially designated as Lemuel V. Bishop-Leroy King Collection in National Library. She asks me convey her respects and deep thanks for your help."

They were silent when he finished reading. At length Danforth called the wine steward to their table and ordered champagne. When it was poured, he lifted his glass.

"I'd like to propose a toast," he said, "a double toast."

"Hear! Hear!" said Helen.

"First," said Danforth, "to Mrs. Cardoni, a gracious, great-hearted lady who richly deserved her good fortune but chose to give it up for patriotic and generous reasons."

"Mrs. Cardoni!" they all said, and drank.

"And second," continued Danforth, "let's drink to Leroy King and his charming wives who, though nothing but humble writers of detective fiction, have managed for once in their lives to give some genuinely great literature to the world!"

They drained their glasses.

The Hong Kong Jewel Mystery

Although they had collaborated in the writing of scores of best-selling detective novels, only once in their career did King Danforth and Martin Leroy themselves become the victims of an actual crime. This was in Hong Kong, during an around-the-world vacation trip with their wives aboard the cruise ship *Valhalla*. And the incident permitted them, much to their delight, to try for the first time their deductive wings, hitherto tested only in theoretical flight, against the bracing air of reality.

The *Valhalla* arrived in Hong Kong Harbor in the early morning. As soon as she docked at Kowloon, and the gangplank was run up to B Deck, Leroy and Danforth, with their wives, immediately went ashore. They spent a pleasant morning sightseeing on the mainland. They ate a superb luncheon of butterfly shrimp and fried rice at the Dragon Inn on the way back from their glimpse of Red China in the New Territories. And they made an extended visit to the establishment of Mr. Gene Pao (pronounced Bow), an excellent Chinese tailor, replenishing their wardrobes at fabulously low prices.

Then, at four o'clock, exhausted by this frenzy of tourist activity, they gratefully returned to the *Valhalla* for a short siesta before dinner. As they walked through the tall iron gate at the end of the pier beside which the ship lay, Leroy said, "Look at that. They're painting the old girl."

Festooned about the ship's vast hull, hanging by ropes and slings everywhere they looked, were chattering Chinese coolies, rapidly applying a coat of fresh white paint to the *Valhalla*.

"There must be at least fifty of them," said Helen Leroy,

impressed.

In their cabin on A Deck, Helen tossed her hat on the bed. Then she pulled off the snap-on earrings she was wearing and opened the top drawer of her dressing table to put them away. In a shocked, incredulous voice she exclaimed, "Oh, no!"

"What's the matter?" Leroy said.

"My jewelry! It's been stolen! Except for what I had on." She gulped. "Look!"

Leroy went over and looked into the drawer. It had been hurriedly ransacked. Helen's small leather jewel case was lying there with its lid open, empty.

Leroy asked, "Everything?"

"Yes. My diamond circle pin. Mother's engagement ring. My sapphire and diamond bracelet. My good earrings." Her voice rose to a wail as she sagged forlornly on the edge of her bed. "Even my gold pin and charm bracelet! What'll we do?"

"Report it. Right away. That's standard procedure." Leroy sprang to the door, snatched it open, and dashed into the corridor. He almost collided with King Danforth who was coming out of his cabin next door.

"Mart!" Danforth cried. "What do you know? Our stateroom's been burgled! Carol's jewelry is gone!"

Leroy slid to a stop. "What? You, too?"

The literary team of "Leroy King" gazed at each other like two auditors who have simultaneously run across evidence of embezzlement in the records of an otherwise blameless charitable institution. Then they grinned at each other. Danforth said, "We're supposed to know how to act in circumstances like these. Come on over and let's kick it around a little, eh?"

"Okay."

Leroy re-entered his room. Helen, who had overheard, was already more cheerful in the knowledge that her misery had congenial company.

Leroy said, "Your good stuff's insured, hon."

"I know. But I can't replace my mother's heirloom ring. Or the bracelet you gave me on our tenth anniversary. They have sentimental value, damn it!" Helen rarely swore. She lifted a hand and brushed back a strand of her honey-colored hair. "Oh, well."

Leroy examined the stateroom. He saw nothing remotely suggesting a clue—except, perhaps, the small indentation in the center of his bed, directly below the open porthole.

Helen said, "If you've solved the mystery, let's go tell Carol and King how it happened." She stood up with a watery smile. "Poor Carol. If they've taken her diamond wrist watch..."

They had. Along with the rest of her jewelry. "Why don't you two experts call the police?" Carol asked.

"Call Charlie Chan," Helen suggested. "Or Mr. Moto. They're the boys for oriental crime, I believe."

"Wait," said Danforth. "Give Leroy King a chance. We want to do this stylishly. Our reputation may well be at stake. Leave us not be hasty."

Helen sat down on Carol's dressing-table stool. "Well, do it stylishly by all means. But do something."

"First," said Leroy, lighting a cigarette and looking at his partner, "as long as we're both insured, we can afford to be cool and objective. So let's think of something intelligent—"

Carol sighed. "Intelligence! At a time like this!" She collapsed on her bunk.

Leroy was looking at Danforth's bed and the porthole above it. "You've got a footprint, too," he said to King, "on the bed under your open porthole. That's how the thief got in, quite obviously. Slid through the porthole, slipped down on the bed, cleaned out the drawers of the dressing table, then stepped up on the bed, and went out the same way."

"Through an opening less than sixteen inches wide?" King questioned.

"Sure. How else? Our doors were locked." Leroy's tone was confident.

"The painters," King murmured tentatively.

"Some of them are certainly small enough to squirm through our portholes," Carol said.

King continued: "It seems the simplest and most logical solution, all right. So let's say it was a painter. A Chinese coolie. That reduces our suspects to a mere fifty or so."

"Fewer than that, King. Only the ones painting in the vicinity of these cabins would have noticed our open portholes and had the chance to duck in and out in a hurry—without being seen by a lot of other coolies."

"Maybe they don't care who sees them," Carol suggested. "Maybe they all compete in a spirit of good clean fun to rob American tourists."

"Don't be bitter," said Danforth. "You are distracting two fine minds from keen assessment of this interesting problem." He rubbed a hand slowly over his hair and began to enjoy himself.

Leroy caught the gleam in his eye and smiled at him. This was a game they had played a thousand times in plotting their books. "What we've got to do," Leroy said, "is discover which painters were nearest our portholes."

"That ought to be easy," Helen offered sweetly. "I'm sure they all speak English."

Carol said, "Call the cops, men. Please. I want my jewelry back. Not just an impersonal insurance check!"

Leroy said, "I wonder what their rules are, over here, regarding bodily search?"

"Search whom?" Carol asked.

"The painters," said Leroy. "There's a big iron gate at the foot of this pier. And it was patrolled by British bobbies when we came through it just now. If they would be willing to search the painters as they go out..."

Danforth glanced at his watch. "Still time if the painters knock off at five o'clock," he said. "Let's go."

Twenty minutes later the purser of the *Valhalla* had reported the theft to the Hong Kong police; the guards at the gate had been alerted and had promised to search every painter as he left the dock; and a Police Department jeep had arrived bearing Detective-Inspector Lo, assigned to their case from the CID office of Tsien Sha Tsin Police Station.

Inspector Lo proved to be a polite, quiet-spoken Chinese in western clothes, with a high, intelligent forehead, a pink scalp that shone through his sparse, combed-back hair, and liquid dark eyes of almost feminine beauty.

"He's darling!" Helen whispered to Carol. "You can have Charlie Chan. I'll take Inspector Lo."

Danforth briefed him skillfully on the robbery. "We took the liberty of asking the dock police to search the painting gang as they leave the ship, Inspector," he finished.

Inspector Lo nodded. "I checked with the dock police when I came onto the pier," he said in excellent English. "All members of the painting gang have now been searched. No jewelry was found, I am sorry to say."

Leroy looked at Danforth, and both shrugged.

Inspector Lo mounted with them to A Deck and carefully examined their staterooms, their portholes, and the deck outside. He held an earnest colloquy in Cantonese with a tan-clad policeman at the end of their corridor. Then he directed a cheerful smile at the dejected faces of Carol and Helen, and said gently, "One of the painting gang. No question about it, ladies. Please leave everything to me."

Dispiritedly, Leroy said, "We were going to Aberdeen for dinner. Any reason why we shouldn't?"

"Go, please, and enjoy yourselves." Inspector Lo paused, then added shyly, "Once the bread is in the oven, it does not need the baker."

"Isn't he a living doll?" Helen breathed.

Inspector Lo departed for the purser's office. Leroy King and his two wives prepared for dinner. The wives, regrettably, did not have their best jewelry to wear with their best dresses.

* * * *

They returned to the ship several hours later, soothed by an impeccably served dinner at the Sea Palace and thrilled by a view of the magic harbor at night—from the observation point high on the peak of Hong Kong island above the clustered lights of Victoria. There was a message in the Leroys' room to call at the purser's office. All four of them hurried down together.

Hansen, the tall Norwegian purser, held out his cupped palm to Helen. "Is this your ring?" he asked.

Her eyes lighted up. "Yes!" she cried. "The tourmaline you bought for me in Rio, Mart! It was one of the things stolen today."

"Where did you find it, Mr. Hansen?" Danforth asked practically.

The purser raised his hands in admiration. "Inspector Lo brought thirty men on board, and they went over every inch of the ship, and then the dock, like mice looking for grains of wheat. This is the only thing they found. It was lying on the dock, Mr. Danforth. About three feet from the edge against which the ship lies, and down toward the gate."

"Let's go and see the place," Helen suggested.

"There's a small circle of white paint at the spot, Mrs. Leroy," said the purser.

They descended the gangplank to the dock and walked along it to where the pier lights revealed a small circle of white paint on the wooden planking. They stood around this visible mark of Inspector Lo's industry and regarded it in silence.

Then King said, "One ring only. On the dock. Nothing on the ship." Leroy nodded slowly. "And look." He pointed. "You can see the pier gate from here. From this spot the thief could have seen the search of his buddies at the gate."

"And he therefore made a quick decision," Danforth said. "He realized he would be caught red-handed, with the jewelry on him. So what does he do?"

Carol groaned aloud. "Don't tell me," she pleaded.

Danforth said, "He gives up any idea of profiting from his robbery the minute he sees the painters are being searched. He gets rid of the jewelry."

"You mean," Helen said in a pained voice, "that he throws all our beautiful watches and rings and bracelets into Hong Kong Harbor?"

"Head of the class, darling," said Leroy. "Probably at this very spot. He just quietly drops the stuff into the water between the ship's side and the edge of the dock."

"What about the tourmaline ring?" Helen asked.

"A near-miss," said Danforth. "When he tossed the stuff into the water, that ring didn't quite make it to the edge of the dock. It hit the pier and stayed on it."

"The beast!" wailed Carol. "Oh, the heartless, dishonest little beast!"

An hour later Inspector Lo found them in the Horseshoe Bar of the *Valhalla*, drinking a farewell toast, in stingers-on-the-rocks, to their lost property. The Inspector bustled in, looking not at all dashed. Quite the contrary. At their invitation he sat down with them.

"The investigation progresses," he announced cheerfully. "No, no drink, thank you. I am too busy. The purser showed you the tourmaline ring?"

They nodded.

Inspector Lo smiled. "It is a clue," he said proudly.

"Some clue," Carol murmured.

"Just an arrow pointing to a watery grave. Isn't that right, Inspector? Didn't the thief throw our jewelry into the harbor?"

"I fear so. But that is no reason to despair."

"What do you mean? Show me a better reason."

"I have already arranged for a deep-sea diving rig and an expert diver. Tomorrow we shall search the bottom of the sea for your jewelry, ladies. The Hong Kong police do not give up easily, you see."

"I'll say you don't," admitted Danforth admiringly. "Any clues as to the guilty painter yet?"

"Not yet. This takes a little time, you understand—even to get a complete list of the painters' names and to look up their records, if any. Then to interrogate fifty of them, to break down the fiber of their group loyalty and personal friendships to the point where they will talk freely of what they have seen or done—" He shrugged. "I have at least done some screening. There are sixteen painters, according to their foreman, who could have robbed you—that is, who had the physical opportunity."

"Sixteen," said Leroy, "is still a lot of suspects."

* * * *

Next morning, when they left the ship to get a fitting of the new clothes they had ordered from the tailor, Mr. Pao, they saw Inspector Lo waving to them from the deck of a small diving barge anchored across the dock from the *Valhalla*. They waved back. When they returned to the ship after luncheon, he intercepted them at the foot of the passenger gangplank. He wore a broad smile on his face and carried a large manila envelope in his hand.

"This is what we have found so far," he said quietly, dumping the envelope's contents into his other hand. He was obviously pleased with himself. "Forty feet down. In two inches of muck."

Incredulously they stared at the collection of jewelry in his hand—until, in honest amazement, Leroy said, "Inspector, you're a genius!"

"No," Lo disclaimed politely, while his eyes glinted with pleasure. "I have a very good diver."

Helen and Carol rapidly catalogued the recovered items.

"And," the Inspector promised gallantly, "we will find more! Trust the Hong Kong Police Department, please."

* * * *

He was as good as his word. By five o'clock his manila envelope contained seventeen of the twenty-five articles that had been stolen from their staterooms. He showed them to the Danforths and Leroys in the latter's cabin. "Tomorrow," he predicted, "we recover the rest."

After he left them, Leroy tapped his fingers against his shadowed jaw, now in need of its second shave of the day. He seemed preoccupied.

"What's bothering you?" Carol asked laughing. "Are you jealous of Inspector Lo?"

Leroy's frown indicated deep thought. "I hate to throw cold water," he said finally, "but one fact leaps to the eye."

"What?"

"Didn't you notice," said Leroy, "that although seventeen of your stolen things have been found, not a single one of the really valuable pieces you lost is among them?"

"All that stuff he just showed us," Danforth supplemented, "was costume jewelry. The inexpensive items."

"Check your lists, girls," Leroy said. "Isn't every one of the still-missing pieces an expensive one? Set with diamonds or sapphires or something obviously quite valuable?"

"Y-e-s," Helen said reluctantly.

"So something is sour," Danforth said, "on the law of averages alone. But what?"

"Not Inspector Lo," Helen said stoutly. "He's a dear, honest detective and I'll stake my life on it. He'll find the rest of our things tomorrow. You'll see."

Leroy rasped his stubble impatiently. "The tourmaline ring, King. It's not very valuable actually, but more so than any of the other items Lo has recovered. Yet they found it on the dock. How come?"

"To make us think just what we did think—and what Inspector Lo still thinks. That all the stuff was thrown into the water, because one of the more valuable pieces was found marking the spot."

"In which case the inevitable conclusion is that the thief threw everything in that wasn't worth much, and kept everything out that he thought really valuable."

"Kept it out? But where?" Helen asked.

"There you have me," Leroy shrugged. "But our clever little coolie probably worked something out."

Danforth said, "Anything a clever coolie can work out, we ought to be able to work out, too. So start thinking, Mart."

"I have," Leroy grinned. "Let's see. The ship has been fine-tooth-combed by Lo and his thirty cops. Right? Ditto the dock. And the painters have all, individually, been carefully searched each time they've left the dock since the robbery. So the thief hasn't carried away the loot; and he hasn't left it hidden on the ship itself or on the dock."

"Brilliant," said Carol. "You're right back where you started. The stuff's in the harbor, that's where."

"No," Leroy said stubbornly. Danforth said, "If he saw his buddies being searched, he'd not only have to think fast, he'd have to act fast, too; wouldn't he?"

"That figures," Leroy said. "He couldn't waste any time looking for a hiding place. It had to be handy, right near where he discovered that the painters were being searched." Suddenly Danforth slapped his thigh with a report like a pistol shot. Helen and Carol jumped. "Hey," said Danforth exuberantly, "what about the most obvious hiding place of all for a painter? In his can of paint?"

"Bingo!" Leroy exclaimed. "I think you've hit it, King. His paint-can would be handy, quick, and practical. And probably be taken off the ship when the painting is finished without the police giving it a second thought."

Danforth reached for the telephone. "Where do you

think the painters leave their equipment overnight?" he said. "Up in the fore peak? Let's ask the purser to have somebody search those paint cans right now.

But after a few eager words with the purser on the telephone, King turned back to them, crestfallen, and slowly replaced the receiver. "Nuts," he said. "The purser says that Inspector Lo had all the paint cans searched yesterday. First thing he did after we left him to go to dinner."

"You're only twenty-four hours behind my favorite detective with that idea," Helen needled them. "Come on, men, you'll have to start thinking again."

Danforth said, "If we're right about his hiding the good pieces of jewelry, he had to hide them before he reached the spot on the dock where the tourmaline ring was found. Right?"

"Right," Leroy agreed. "And that localizes it pretty well. Since the stuff's not on the ship, it's somewhere between our staterooms here and the place where the tourmaline ring was found."

"And the moment he saw the painters being searched at the dock gate," Danforth said, "he knew that his biggest problem was to get his loot ashore without being caught. Obviously, it was going to be impossible before our ship sailed." Danforth rubbed a hand over his head. "So what's the next logical move for him?"

Promptly Leroy replied, "To hide the valuable pieces in some way that would permit him to recover them after the ship has sailed."

"Exactly. So we're looking for a hiding place that's quickly accessible to a departing painter, and guaranteed to be still here after the ship has sailed tomorrow."

"Not on the ship," Leroy mused. "Not on his person. Not on the dock. But how about beside the dock?"

"That's the same old thing," Carol said. "In the water."

"Do you mean...?" Danforth began, but Leroy interrupted him. "Why not in one of the bumpers?"

"Bumpers?" Helen asked, puzzled.

"Sure. You know—those old automobile tires they hang down the side of the dock to act as fenders when a ship comes alongside?"

"That," said Danforth, jumping to his feet, "is a very interesting possibility. Lo's men could have overlooked them, with the ship's side actually resting against some of them. Let's go and look for ourselves. Bring a flashlight, Carol, will you?"

They trooped out of the ship onto the dock. It was a balmy evening. The velvety darkness of the harbor was laced with the moving lights of the Kowloon-Victoria ferries. The oily harbor water glinted and winked between garish banks of neon advertising signs. Hong Kong's sharp, acid, not unpleasant smell filled the night air.

With the aid of Carol's flashlight they carefully examined all the tire-fenders hanging on both sides of the dock and far forward as the spot where the tourmaline ring had been found. They found nothing.

Leroy shook his head sadly. "We're getting old, pal," he said to Danforth. "Maybe Leroy King should retire and live on his royalties."

"Good idea," Carol said jauntily. "And to begin with, who's for a martini?" She and Carol turned back.

In the *Valhalla*'s Horseshoe Bar, Danforth said in an insistent though disgruntled voice, "That jewelry's out there some place! I know it. Hidden in something that will still be here after the ship sails tomorrow."

"In the water," Carol murmured. "Just as Inspector Lo believes."

Danforth muttered to himself and started to take a sip of his cocktail. Suddenly, in mid-swallow, he choked. He put his drink down on the bar so abruptly that it spilled. "Mart!" he said. "How do the painters leave the ship when they knock off work at night?"

For a moment Leroy stared. "By Jove!" he said, then, his

eyes widening. "The very place!"

Danforth coughed and rushed on, "The ship normally uses its own, but here it must be part of the port facilities."

"And therefore it stays here when the ship has sailed," Leroy finished.

"And from there the thief could have seen his buddies being searched at the dock gate."

"What are you two talking about?" asked Carol plaintively.

She received no answer. For the other cruise passengers in the ship's bar were at that moment treated to the sight of Leroy and Danforth abandoning their drinks and running from the room, followed more sedately by their puzzled wives.

Helen and Carol found their husbands standing on B Deck at the top of the gangplank. This cleated wooden walkway, that led from B Deck down to the dock, was bordered on cither side by waist-high handrails made of three-inch aluminum pipe. The upper ends of these pipes were stopped with polished teak wood plugs—like finials at the top of two horizontal flagpoles.

Without a word Danforth laid a hand on one of the plugs and twisted it gently. It was not fitted tightly into the pipe and came off easily in his hand. He stopped and peered into the end of the hollow handrail. "Nothing," he said to Leroy.

Leroy turned to Carol and Helen before he tried the handrail plug on his side of the gangplank. "If you want your jewelry back," he said, "look in there, ladies." He pulled out the teakwood finial from the second handrail.

Helen stooped over and applied an eye to the hollow pipe. When she stepped back, Carol took her place. They looked at each other for a moment and then Carol said, "Now who's your favorite detective, Helen?"

Helen answered, "Leroy King. Who else?"

For the rest of the jewels were there.

* * * *

Later Inspector Lo said, "We shall arrest the thief after your ship sails, when he returns to the dock to recover his loot from this gangplank railing. So you see, you have not only found your jewels, you have caught the thief as well."

"Poor lamb!" said Helen, beginning to feel sorry for the unknown coolie. "All those long years in jail!"

"His sentence should not exceed one year," Lo said quietly.

"What?" said Danforth. "Only one year for grand larceny?"

Lo nodded. "If this thief had succeeded in his robbery, he would have been a rich man," he said. "But since he failed, he still wins second prize, as it were. A jail sentence."

"This is a prize?" Carol asked, confused.

"To be sure. In jail he will have shelter, leisure, companionship, and three good meals a day. That's far better than he can possibly live outside on a painter's wage, you see. And that's why the judge will give him only one year of this pleasant punishment although he deserves more."

Inspector Lo spread his hands in an oriental gesture. "For men like this lazy painter, a jail sentence is luxury living. In fact, my friends, here in Hong Kong,"—Inspector Lo smiled shyly—"many of our criminals refer to prison as 'The American Way of Life!'"

The Tahitian Powder Box Mystery

From a porthole on the *Valhalla*'s sundeck a bare, slender, human arm suddenly appeared, thrust outward from the shoulder. The hand at the end of the arm tilted a round shallow box and dumped the contents casually into the purple swells that sucked at the ship's seaward side as she lay alongside the dock in Papeete.

Then the arm withdrew, having first paused briefly to tap the cardboard container against the ship's side and thus dislodge the final clinging grains of the box's contents.

Nobody saw this happen the first time.

But on the upper sundeck, directly above the porthole, the Danforths and Leroys stood at the ship's rail, raptly regarding the spectacular Tahitian sunset that was now painting the sky behind Moorea with gold and vermilion. And Helen Leroy, sniffing delicately, said, "You may not believe it, but this is absolutely the first perfumed sunset I ever saw. Or smelled, rather."

"Perfumed?" her husband asked absently, watching the changing colors of sky and sea.

"Yes, perfumed. Don't you smell it?"

"I do," Carol Danforth said, also sniffing. "And it's not any cheap, tawdry, domestic perfume, either. That's Chanel Number Five in my opinion. And my opinion is pretty expert!"

King Danforth said, "Are you out of your mind? Tahiti is reputedly romantic, I admit. But perfumed sunsets!"

"I smell it, too," Leroy said with surprise. "Take a deep breath, King. The girls are right."

Danforth followed instructions. "So l smell something nice," he conceded. "Flowers on the island perhaps? Frangipani? Jasmine?"

"That's Chanel Number Five," Carol insisted. And sneezed.

Martin Leroy sneezed, too. "Chanel, maybe," he said then, "but powder, not perfume. Look. That's what's making us sneeze."

He pointed to a mist of fine particles being lifted in a fragrant cloud over the rail by a gentle updraft of the sunset breeze.

Danforth said, "Somebody must be jettisoning bath powder out of her porthole somewhere below us."

"Who'd throw away Chanel powder, I'd like to know?" Helen said indignantly. "Let me look." She stretched up on her toes and leaned out over the rail. They all stared downward.

As they watched, an arm and hand emerged from the porthole below them and emptied the contents of a box into the sea. A light cloud of powder quickly dispersed on the air. When the arm withdrew, Leroy said, "That's one way to cut your inventory in a hurry."

"If you don't care about your overhead," quipped Danforth as Leroy sneezed once more.

"I think it's a vulgar gesture," Helen said. "Why not just quietly put the box of powder in her cabin wastebasket if she wants to get rid of it?" She turned to Carol. "I wonder who she is?"

Carol tossed her dark head. "I'll count the portholes from the back of the ship and find out," she said.

"Later," Danforth interposed. He glanced at his watch. "We've got to get moving. The dinner tour for Les Tropiques is supposed to gather on the dock right now."

"Then let's go," Leroy said with enthusiasm. "We don't want to miss the dancing girls!"

* * * *

The Tahitian dancing girls were very good. Even Helen and Carol admired their grace, sinuosity, and curiously Caucasian beauty. And the dinner at Les Tropiques restaurant was very good, too.

Their table was set in a corner of the wide terrace that faced the lagoon. As they ate, darkness gradually dimmed the outlines of the terrace and hid the faint line of white surf breaking over the reef, far out. Down the coast to their right, festive strings of colored lights marked the *Valhalla* at her pier. At full dark, natives with torches in their hands came and lighted oil lamps around the edges of the terrace to illuminate the wild, hip-swaying movements of the Tahitian dance troupe.

Danforth breathed a sigh of purest satisfaction and said, "I never thought I'd live to see the day that a travel folder understated the case for a tourist attraction."

"I take it you like Tahiti," Helen said, laughing. She looked at the dancers in their grass skirts and straw bras, their bare golden flesh burnished by the leaping flare of the oil lamps, and she smiled at Carol.

"Like it?" said Danforth. "It gets me right here." He tapped his chest.

John Rich, a fellow passenger from the *Valhalla*, was sitting at the next table with three loquacious widows. He leaned over and said with a grin, "I heard that, Mr. Danforth. And how right you are! Isn't this great?" Rich was a bachelor, slim, dark-eyed, fortyish, with formal good manners but a slightly raffish air. He was very popular with the *Valhalla* passengers, especially the unattached women. It was rumored he had been the chauffeur-houseman of a recently deceased Detroit industrialist who had remembered him generously in his will. This cruise, the ship's gossip ran, was in the nature of a celebration of his newfound independence.

Leroy replied, "It's great, all right. We can't afford to go too far overboard, though—not with our wives sitting here with us!"

Rich laughed and indicated his table companions. "I haven't got a wife," he said, "but my harem, here, is trying to make me put on the brakes. I've already warned them that I'm striking out on my own right after dinner!"

"Good hunting," Leroy said.

The dinner party broke up just then in a burst of applause for the native dancers.

* * * *

Quinn's, the most famous saloon in the South Seas, was a madhouse when they arrived some time later. Almost every able-bodied passenger from the *Valhalla* was there, it seemed, and a raucous mob of French, Polynesians, Melanesians, Orientals, and mixtures thereof swelled the uproar. Everybody in the place appeared to be either laughing shrilly, shouting for drinks, beating beer glasses on the scarred table tops, singing drunkenly, or publicly romancing the unashamed native B-girls.

The Danforths and Leroys found a table as far from the bar as possible and ordered stingers.

They were no sooner seated than Carol said, "There's John Rich over there."

They looked across the wide room and saw John Rich standing at the end of the bar. He was talking to a barefooted Polynesian girl clad in a low-cut island dress of figured red cotton. The girl's long straight hair poured down her back like a black waterfall.

"He's found himself a Polynesian houri, I see," Leroy said dreamily. "And not bad, either!"

Danforth said, "You know what? That girl with Rich is one of the girls who were selling flowers on the porch of Les Tropiques when we came out."

"You must have studied her with considerable care to be able to recognize her across a mad place like this at forty paces," Helen teased him. "For the life of me, I can't see what's so terribly attractive to you men about bare feet and long straight black hair." Helen was an ethereally lovely blonde.

"Bare feet!" Leroy laughed. "Are her feet bare, too?"

Danforth said, "She reminds me of something."

"Of what?" This was from Carol. "Whistler's mother?"

With studied restraint Danforth answered, "No, but something rather curious. After dinner I waited on the porch of Les Tropiques while you three visited the washrooms, remember? John Rich came out of the restaurant while I was waiting. He stopped on the porch and said something to that girl he's with over there. She was selling flowers then."

"Asking her for a date," said Helen. "He said he was going a-wolfing. What's strange about that?"

"He was speaking Italian," Danforth said softly.

"Italian?" Leroy raised his eyebrows. "You sure?"

"Or Latin."

"John Rich speaking Latin?" Carol hooted.

"Maybe his real name is Ricci," Leroy hazarded, "in which case he might know Italian."

"True," said Danforth. "But what about the girl? Would she know Italian?"

"What makes you think she did?"

"She understood him—at least, she answered him without a moment's pause. In English. But the last word of Rich's question to her—that's all I heard—was definitely not in English. It was either Italian or Latin."

"What was the last word?"

"Acuminata. That's what he said. With a rising inflection, hence a question."

Leroy slapped the table and laughed. "I've always told you, King, if you want to be a well-rounded mystery novelist you should learn a little about everything—including botany. Only a modicum, mind you, but something about the flowers and fruits and—er—flora of our teeming planet."

"What are you drinking, Mart?" Helen asked sweetly. "Ambrosia? The birds and the bees will be next, no doubt."

"And I can't think of a better place than Tahiti for that lecture!" Carol added.

"Why flora, Mart?" said Danforth.

"And why not Cora, Dora, and Nora, if it comes to that?" Carol laughed.

"Because," Leroy pointed out patiently, "if you knew anything about the flora of these islands, King, you'd recognize that the Italian word you overheard John Rich using was merely a descriptive adjective, part of the botanical name for a genus of the frangipani plant."

"You're kidding," Danforth said.

"Not at all. I believe the full term is plumeria acuminata—meaning the sharp or pointed frangipani. White. As distinguished, let us say, from plumeria rubra, which is simply red jasmine flowers to us learned botanists." Leroy preened himself.

His wife exclaimed in astonishment, "Why, Mart, you never told me you knew so much about flowers! Will you address our garden club when you get home?"

"Gladly." Leroy bowed. "You can sign me up now by buying me another drink."

"Wait a minute," Danforth protested. He rubbed a hand over his crew-cut. "So Rich wasn't speaking Italian. But I still think it was odd for Rich to ask about the pointed frangipani, or whatever you called it, by its scientific name, don't you?"

Leroy nodded seriously. "You wouldn't think the average retired-type chauffeur from Detroit would know there was such a thing as frangipani, let alone what its correct botanical designation is."

Helen, who had been watching Rich across the saloon, spoke up. "New song title: 'He asked for plumeria acuminata, but he got red jasmine instead.' That lei around his neck is woven of pink flowers."

"If you would only let me finish," Danforth said, "I can explain that, too. In answer to Rich's question about acuminata, that girl over there stood up from among the flower sellers on the restaurant porch and said to Rich, 'Good evening, Monsieur, wouldn't you like this better?' And she hung that red jasmine lei around his neck, and they went off together, arm in arm."

"Just like that?" Helen asked.

"Just like that. So she picked him up, if you want my opinion, not the other way around."

"The hussy!" said Carol, waving across the room to John Rich and his companion. "How fascinating! Maybe they will join us."

She invited them to do so in vigorous sign language. Rich said something to the native girl in the red dress. She shook her head and turned back to the bar. Rich spread his hands in apology to Carol, then put his arm around the girl's bare shoulders. She turned a cool, remote smile on him then. But she seemed to be looking beyond him toward the door.

* * * *

For the next two days King Danforth and Martin Leroy, known to millions of mystery story fans as the author, "Leroy King," were so completely occupied with sightseeing and shopping in Tahiti that neither they nor their wives gave another thought to plumeria acuminata or Chanel Number Five bath powder.

It wasn't until the *Valhalla* was steaming out of Papeete harbor bound for Suva in the Fijis, that Carol Danforth, sipping her pre-prandial gimlet, said, "And now that we're back to normal shipboard scandal, I'm still curious to know who was throwing away Chanel bath powder the other day."

"I'm astonished at your ladylike patience," Leroy commented. "I thought you'd have found out who she was long since."

Danforth lit a cigarette. "One thing is fairly obvious," he said idly, but with a challenging glance at his partner. "She isn't just an amateur powder-dumper, this gal. She's a professional."

"How do you reach that obscure conclusion?" Leroy asked.

"It leaps to the eye. The lady didn't throw away just one boxful of powder. She threw away at least two. That makes her a pro, doesn't it?"

Carol said, "What do you mean, she threw away two boxes of powder?"

"Remember you smelled the powder while we were watching the sunset? And saw some of it blowing over the rail? And sneezed because of it?"

"Yes."

"Well, that means she had already dumped one box of powder before the one we saw her dump. Because we didn't look down till afterward."

"Elementary," Leroy murmured. His expressive face lit up with the pleasure he always felt when engaging in this kind of deductive play with his partner. "But something else about the incident seemed of even more significance to me, if I may say so."

Danforth grinned. "Please say so."

"Cut it out, you two," Carol said plaintively. "You can't make a mystery out of this, not even in fun. I forbid it. We're on vacation. All I want to know is who the silly woman is who throws away Chanel Number Five powder."

"Please," Leroy said with an air of injured dignity, "doesn't anyone want to know what I deduced?"

"Of course, darling." Helen patted his hand. "Because I'm going to hear it anyway. But please make it short."

"Very well. I deduced that whoever was throwing away the powder wanted the empty box for another purpose. She didn't throw the whole package into the sea—just the powder."

"A sobering thought," Danforth acknowledged. "What could she want with two empty powder boxes?"

Helen laughed. "Maybe she wanted something to keep her old buttons and pins in. Or her false teeth at night."

"A distinct possibility," her husband said approvingly.

Abruptly, Carol said, "Pardon me a moment."

She went over and spoke to the bartender who smiled and handed her something from under the bar. She came back with what proved to be a deck plan of the *Valhalla*, showing all staterooms, portholes, showers, closets, bars, and other features of the ship.

"Now, then," Carol went on in a businesslike tone, "the porthole from which the powder-dumper was operating was the eighth from the stern." She carefully counted eight portholes from the rear of the ship's sundeck. "She lives in cabin S-34," Carol announced triumphantly.

"I'll run down to the Purser's Office and look at the list of cabins," Helen offered eagerly. "Then we'll know who she is."

Within five minutes Helen returned, obviously bursting with news. "It isn't a woman at all!" she said. "How do you like that?"

"You mean there's no woman listed in Stateroom S-34?"

"Not one. It's a single cabin occupied exclusively by..." She paused dramatically. "By our bachelor friend, Mr. John Rich."

Leroy slowly put his drink down and straightened in his chair. His eyes met Danforth's. "A visiting lady, then?" he asked. "One of those widows he calls his 'harem'? Could that be the one who was dumping bath powder from his porthole?"

Danforth shook his head, frowning. "Not likely. But John Rich is small-boned, slender, and he has small hands. That bare arm from the porthole could have been his."

Leroy rubbed his jaw. "Well, well, well," he said softly,

almost to himself. "If that's true, we have two incidents in which Mr. John Rich acted quite out of character—dumping powder into the ocean from his stateroom porthole, and using familiarly the scientific name of a tropical flower he shouldn't even know exists."

"Lots of people have flowers for a hobby, possibly exchauffeurs..." Helen began, but both men ignored her. They were suddenly as hot on the scent of this little mystery as though it were one of their own fictional plots.

"Suppose," said Leroy, "it was John Rich dumping bath powder, where would he have got it?"

"Right here on the ship," Carol said. "The shop sells French perfume, soap, and powder at very low prices."

"Say he bought the powder on the ship, then. Why?"

"Not for gifts to take home," Danforth said, "because he threw the stuff away. Therefore, he must have wanted empty powder boxes."

"Exactly. Again, why?"

"To hold something else, as you brilliantly deduced."

"But why buy expensive Chanel and waste it, just to get empty boxes? Why not the cheapest possible brand?"

"Ah," said Danforth, smiling, "one can but guess as to that. My guess is that Rich wants somebody—perhaps the customs officials in New York at the end of this cruise—to think he's bringing home a few gift boxes of Chanel powder, when he's really bringing home something else."

"Now that," Leroy grinned, "is a truly brilliant hypothesis to which I subscribe whole-heartedly. Respectable Chanel powder containers would be smuggling camouflage of the highest order for whatever John Rich fills them with."

Helen said in a resigned tone, "The next question before the house, therefore, is this: What does John Rich intend to fill the powder boxes with?"

"I withdraw my suggestion about buttons and pins," Helen volunteered.

"Thank you." Danforth swung one leg over the arm of his chair. "Since he was emptying the boxes at Papeete, one might reasonably assume that he meant to fill them with something he intended to get in Tahiti."

"Any ideas?" Leroy asked.

"Dancing girls," said Carol. "Think how the boys would go for Tahitian bunnies in our key clubs at home!"

"Be serious," Leroy rebuked her. "Great minds are at work here. And your frivolity impedes smooth cerebration. Well, King?"

Danforth shrugged. "Whatever it was, I'll wager the flower girl who picked him up at Les Tropiques had something to do with it."

Leroy started visibly. He said with a trace of excitement, "That's it, by Jove!"

"What's it?" Helen demanded.

"I'll bet John Rich was using a prearranged recognition signal when he went through that plumeria acuminata bit—to identify himself to the flower girl."

"Of course!" Danforth tapped his fingers nervously on the table. "And the flower girl gives him a prearranged response and the red jasmine lei as the other half of the signal. That's why they became old buddies immediately and were in Quinn's together. They had some kind of deal cooking."

"Sex appeal alone drew them together, if you want to know what I think," Carol said. "I could tell by the way Rich looked at her!"

"But not," Leroy said thoughtfully, "by the way she looked at him. She kept brushing off Rich's passes at the bar and watching Quinn's door as though she were expecting someone."

"Her principal, you mean?" said Danforth. "The boss smuggler, maybe? You think she was assigned to pick Rich out of our tourist group and take him to her leader at Quinn's?"

"Something like that makes sense." Leroy absent-mindedly reached over and finished his wife's gimlet.

"Now that you've had your cocktail, darling," his wife said with deceptive sweetness, "it's well past dinner time. Come on. Forget John Rich, please. There's roast reindeer tonight."

Danforth and Leroy docilely followed their wives to the dining room.

* * * *

With the last bite of dessert, however—something their Norwegian table steward referred to as "peaches pie"—the two mystery writers returned to their speculations.

"Tahiti," Leroy ruminated aloud, "produces nothing much but breadfruit, mangoes, taro root, copra, girls, climate, and leisure, not necessarily in that order. And none of these would fit comfortably into a Chanel powder box."

"It occurred to me during the reindeer steak," said Danforth, "that Tahiti may be merely a way station, a pickup point, for whatever it is that Rich is smuggling."

"It's isolated enough, all right. In the middle of the Pacific, halfway between Asia and everywhere else. Let's see. Asia. From Asia, one smuggles embroideries and jade originating in Red China, oriental workmen who will work elsewhere for peanuts—"

Danforth snapped his fingers. "Why not the obvious answer?"

Politely Leroy inquired, "And what is the obvious answer, Professor? As if we didn't know."

"Think of boxes full of white powder. Think of Red China. Think of—"

"Heroin?"

"What else?"

"From the beginning," Leroy murmured, "it seemed clearly indicated."

Carol lifted her eyes to the ceiling and said, "You poor,

mystery-happy idiots!"

Danforth ignored her. "There's more than a chance, Mart," he said, "that John Rich is not a retired chauffeur, but a member of some dope-peddling organization in the United States. He takes this round-the-world cruise solely for the purpose of picking up a shipment of heroin in Tahiti, where—by equally devious means—it has arrived from Hong Kong or Red China. Rich is seemingly above suspicion—an innocent tourist on a cruise."

Leroy took it up. "Right. Rich identifies himself to his Tahitian colleagues as the courier sent from America to pick up the heroin, by an exchange of prearranged code phrases with the flower girl, of which plumeria acuminata is undoubtedly one. After he has identified himself, the heroin is passed to him—perhaps in Quinn's—where the confusion would cover up any monkey business. Rich then conceals the heroin in the Chanel powder boxes he has prepared in his cabin.

"At the end of the cruise he calmly carries the heroin through customs, having dutifully entered several gift boxes of Chanel Number Five powder on his customs declaration, all according to regulations. The heroin powder in genuine Chanel boxes would almost certainly go undetected, even by a careful inspection which, incidentally, returning cruise passengers arc seldom subjected to. Is that it?"

"That's exactly it," Danforth said. "So let's go ask the Captain to have Rich's cabin searched for the heroin. If it's there, the Captain can tip the Narcotics and Customs Bureaus by radio-telephone and have them catch Rich red-handed as he comes ashore in New York."

Leroy turned to Carol and Helen. "Will you excuse us?" he asked. "We'll meet you in the toward lounge later." He and Danforth stood up.

Helen said, "Are you really going to Captain Hansen with that crazy story?"

"Certainly," her husband answered. "As conscientious

American citizens..."

"But it's completely fantastic!" Carol broke in. "From an empty powder box and the name of a tropical flower, you deduce an international dope ring operating on this ship! Now really!"

"We didn't make a mystery out of this thing," Leroy defended himself. "We've merely made logical deductions from observed facts, that's all."

Carol and Helen looked at each other and suddenly dissolved in laughter.

"What's so funny?" Leroy asked.

"You!" his wife managed to gasp through her laughter. "You and your 'observed facts'! That's what's funny!" She and Helen struggled to contain their mirth. "But you're perfectly right when you say that you and King didn't make a mystery out of this."

"He did," Helen crowed.

Slowly Danforth and Leroy resumed their seats. They watched their wives like wary baby-sitters observing unfamiliar and obstreperous charges.

"Don't be cross with us, darlings," Carol said, "but one of the facts on which you based your deductions was slightly wrong. And it's our fault."

"What fact?" Leroy spoke sharply.

"The number of the cabin from which the arm dumped the powder out the porthole."

"It wasn't S-34?"

"No. It was S-36."

"You said it was the eighth porthole from the stern," Leroy reminded her.

"I know. But it really wasn't. I fibbed. It was the ninth."

Danforth said to Helen, "And you looked it up and told us it was occupied, that cabin, by John Rich!" He looked at her accusingly. "What for?"

"Just for laughs," Helen chortled. "To see what you master-plotters would make of it. And you haven't disappointed us one bit, have they, Carol?"

Danforth summoned a rueful grin. "These women we call our wives," he said to his partner, "call powerfully to mind a single old-fashioned word: perfidious."

Leroy nodded. "At the very least," he agreed. Then he asked his wife curiously, "Who does occupy cabin S-36 if John Rich doesn't?"

"Two of the widows in John Rich's 'harem' occupy it—the cabin is a double."

"And it was one of them who threw away the powder?"

"They had each," Carol explained, "bought a box of Chanel Number Five powder for use on this trip from the shop. But Mrs. Piggott, the older of the two, proved allergic to Chanel powder. It made her sneeze dreadfully. So she threw the powder out the porthole."

"And her roommate?"

"She very obligingly threw hers out, too, since she couldn't use it without causing Mrs. Piggott distress. And she'd already opened her box."

"But why save the boxes?"

Carol laughed. "Mrs. Piggott is going to the masquerade ball tomorrow night as a typical cruise shopper, with bargain items she's bought on this trip draped all over her. She decided the two empty powder boxes would make a good addition to her masquerade costume. So she saved them to wear."

"Well, well," Leroy murmured. His lean face, surprisingly, reflected pride and affection rather than anger as he contemplated his wife's duplicity. "When did you find all this out?" he asked curiously.

"In the ladies' washroom at Les Tropiques after dinner that night," Helen said. "You know how girls talk in places like that! And there was some powder there that made Mrs. Piggott sneeze, which got her started on the subject."

"And I suppose," said Danforth with an injured air, "you also knew all about Rich's use of plumeria acuminata to the flower girl on the porch?"

Helen said, "Mrs. Piggott used to be a botany teacher, didn't you know? As a member of John Rich's 'harem,' I'm sure she had talked to him on some of the local Tahitian blooms. And I guess John Rich just used the plumeria name to show off to the half-naked flower girl—you know, impress her with the fact that he knew something about Tahiti."

Carol said, "I told you it was sex appeal alone that drew them together."

"Very likely." Leroy called the wine steward and ordered a B & B for each of them. When it came, he looked over his tiny glass at his partner and remarked with a grin. "Well, King, even if we were wrong about it, I wouldn't say we completely wasted our time on this powder box mystery, would you?"

"By no means," Danforth replied sardonically. "Far from it. Just think, I shall never again be ignorant of the proper name tor a pointed white frangipani flower! This is not to be lightly regarded."

"I didn't mean that," Leroy said. "I meant that we've been forcibly brought face to face in this business with the greatest enigma of them all—with the only mystery that even Leroy King may never be able to solve."

Helen and Carol dropped their eyes modestly. Carol kicked Helen under the table. "I think they mean us," she said wickedly. "Aren't they cute?"

The Zanzibar Shirt Mystery

"Next village," the black Arab driver announced in barely intelligible English, "is name Bububu."

Helen Leroy said, "He's joking!"

King Danforth was consulting a map of Zanzibar. "Incredible as it sounds," he said, "the next village is Bububu."

"That's not a name," Martin Leroy said. "That's the way Bing Crosby used to start his theme song."

Carol Danforth touched a hand to her dark hair and sniffed through the broken window of the ancient sedan in which they were riding. "M-m-m!" she said softly. "Isn't that heavenly? What a lovely smelling place!"

"If you like the smell of cloves," her husband said, also sniffing the perfumed air.

"I happen to prefer the smell of Hershey, Pennsylvania," Leroy said, grinning. "It's chocolate-flavored, rather than clove. But I'll grant you, Zanzibar smells pretty good."

Their cruise ship, *Valhalla*, had dropped anchor that morning in Zanzibar harbor, and her complement of touring Americans had hastened ashore to sightsee the fabulous spice island off the coast of East Africa. The Leroys and the Danforths, after an hour in the narrow, crowded, dirty streets of Zanzibar city, had elected to hire a car and take a circular tour of the island, away from the souvenir hawkers and the overpowering scents of the town.

"That's an extremely provocative name, Bububu," Leroy said in a rapt voice. "It's put me in a lyrical frame of mind."

"Spare us, darling," his wife said affectionately. "No poetry, please. It's too hot."

"When it comes over me, it comes over me, baby." Leroy winked at Danforth. "Listen:

"I love you, and I'd follow you
From Zanzibar to Bububu—"

"Oh, a love poem," Helen conceded, pleased. "That's different. Please go on."

King said, "African place names! May I add a couplet?"

"Feel free. Be my guest."

So Danforth intoned:

"From Machadadorp, or even Cuba,
"I'd trail you to Mtubatuba."

"Great!" Leroy said, and added:

"And we'd build a little cottage cozy
On the swampy banks of Umfalozi—"

"All right, knock it off," Carol interrupted inelegantly. "Here's Bububu."

"Some village," Helen said. "Two houses!"

The driver pulled up under an enormous coconut palm, turned off his wheezing engine, and said with a spacious gesture, "Bububu."

On the dilapidated building beside the car, a sign bore the faded letters: Post Office—Bububu. Through the glassless windows, they could see that the building was falling into ruin and completely deserted.

"No one live here," the driver explained. "No need post office."

"That figures," said Danforth looking around him. "How about that building over there, Ali? What's the red rooster on the wall mean?"

"Rooster mean hotel."

"Whew!" Carol breathed. "I can smell it from here, right through the cloves!" She fanned herself with her handkerchief. "Let's stay in the car, Helen."

Danforth and Leroy got out of the car, sweating in the sticky tropical heat. Together they strolled across the road to inspect the hotel. It had only one ground-floor room, open across the front. Inside was a packed-mud floor, indescribably filthy; a rickety zinc-topped table stood in a near corner with two chairs beside it; an untidy shelf displayed three bottles—evidently the hotel's bar; and at the back of the room a stairway ascended uncertainly to an upper floor where, presumably, a bedroom waited to welcome the weary traveler.

For the moment, however, it looked as if two weary travelers had decided to pass up the bedroom for the bar. Huddled under the liquor shelf on the mud floor slept a short, dirty-robed Arab, breathing in long, phlegmy snores. The bartender? And seated on one of the chairs by the table, with his head and arms sprawled helplessly in a puddle of spilled liquor on the table top, was a second man, quite obviously a white man. He wore a very loud sports shirt and he was dead drunk. There was an overturned liquor bottle, empty, on the table near where his cheek rested.

"That boy is well and truly bagged," Danforth said, grinning. "White man's burden got too heavy for him, I guess. Makes me think of Gauguin and Tahiti and the decay of the tropics."

He took his Polaroid camera off his shoulder, aimed it at the drunken patron of the Red Rooster Hotel, focused and snapped a picture, his wink light flashing. "I've got to have record of this. A mood piece, a tropical tone poem."

Leroy wrinkled his nose. "Why do you suppose he picked a God-forsaken place like this to do his drinking in?"

"Who knows?" Danforth checked his watch, then stripped the finished print from his camera. "I'll show this to the girls. Make them glad they stayed in the car. Anything else you want to see here?"

"Let's go. I need some of that clove-scented air, after this." They turned and walked back to their car. "There's another car," Leroy said idly, "behind the hotel. It's even more ancient than ours."

"Nobody in it," Danforth said. "Must belong to the drunk."

They reached their own car. Leroy said, "We've got a punch line for you, girls."

"You'll never make your dreams come true
By buying booze in Bububu!"

They climbed into the car and Danforth exhibited the photograph. The driver headed back to the city on a narrow, paved road lined with feathery clove trees, tall palms, and broad-leaved banana plants.

Carol took one look at the Polaroid picture of Bububu's drunken hotel guest and exclaimed in a startled voice, "Why, that's Harry Gardiner, King!"

Her husband stared at her. "Harry Gardiner? You mean, from the ship? Are you cracking up, dear?"

Helen leaned over and looked at the print. "Of course, it's Harry Gardiner," she said sharply. "Carol's right."

Danforth glanced at Leroy and shrugged. "What makes you think so?"

"The sports shirt," Helen said confidently. "What else? I'd recognize it anywhere." She tapped the picture. "There's only one shirt like that in the whole world. Literally. And it belongs to Harry Gardiner on our ship."

Danforth said in astonishment, "It's just a loud shirt. There must be thousands like it."

"Oh, no, there aren't! Harry had that shirt made especially for him when we were in Tahiti on this cruise—from a bolt of cloth freshly loomed by a left-handed princess or something. He told us all about it. And the princess absolutely guaranteed there was no other shirt in the whole world exactly like it—it was a brand-new material, never on the market before. She designed it herself. Harry bought the whole bolt."

"The old sales pitch," Danforth said. "Exclusive shirt, jack up the price."

"No." Leroy looked thoughtful. "I remember something about it, too, now you mention it, Helen. The shirt was an original. Unique. One of a kind. Didn't Harry show you a written guarantee to that effect?"

"He certainly did. Passion flowers and frangipani blossoms entwined in a crazy pattern on a brown and gold background. There couldn't be another like it—certainly not here in Zanzibar, on the other side of the world from Tahiti."

"It has to be Harry," Carol said, "in your picture." She clicked her tongue against her teeth in disapproval. "And I thought Harry didn't drink! How wrong can you be?"

"I tell you, the guy wasn't Harry Gardiner," King said. "It was some local drunk wearing a shirt just like Harry's, that's all."

"All we saw was the top of his head," Leroy demurred.

"And his arms," Danforth pointed out. "On top of the table. Look." He pointed to his snapshot. "See his left arm? A tattoo big as an apple on his forearm. Anchor and snake. Does Harry Gardiner have a tattoo on his left arm?"

"No-o-o," Helen admitted grudgingly, "he hasn't. I'd have noticed it in the swimming pool."

"So it's not Harry," Danforth said. "Q.E.D. Or, if you still doubt it, let's go back and pull his face out of the schnapps puddle and make sure."

"Oh, no!" Carol protested. "Even if it was Harry, we have no right to do that—after all, it's none of our business, not really."

"I'm glad that's settled." Danforth leaned back against the car's torn upholstery. "Old Harry would love to know you thought he's plastered in Bububu. A teetotaler like him!"

"I still say there's only one shirt in the whole world like his," Helen murmured. "So maybe somebody stole it from him. After all, he's a bachelor, you know, with no wife to look after his wardrobe."

Leroy hooted. "Poor Harry! No wife. Only three million dollars of Texas oil money at the tender age of thirty-two! Nothing to do but take leisurely cruises around the world on luxury ships, paying his cousin Justin's fare, just for company and kicks."

"And not likely to be soaking up Zanzibar booze in a filthy tavern in Bububu," Danforth finished. "Is he?"

They were forced to admit that it was most unlikely. But they agreed not to hurt Harry's feelings by telling him the grim news that a drunk on Zanzibar Island owned a passion flower-frangipani shirt exactly like the one he thought was guaranteed to be exclusively his.

* * * *

At 6:30 that evening, with the sun's golden disk dropping spectacularly behind the Sultan's white-arcaded palace on the waterfront, the *Valhalla* sailed majestically out of Zanzibar harbor. The Danforths and the Leroys sat in the Horseshoe Bar, languidly sipping preprandial gimlets, pleasantly wearied by the day's excursion ashore.

All at once Martin Leroy said softly, as though to himself, "Suppose it was Harry Gardiner's shirt on that drunk?"

Helen and Carol looked at him blankly. But Danforth slowly sat up straighter in his chair, his lanky body tense. "You've been thinking about it, too," he said.

"Couldn't shake it. We both know that wasn't Harry Gardiner. And there must be other shirts like his. But just suppose it was his shirt."

Carol spoke up before her husband could answer. "I know that tone, Mart," she admonished gently. "You two are plotting a mystery again!"

"Why not?" Leroy asked innocently. "It's our business, after all."

A speculative gleam appeared in Helen's sapphire eyes. She spoke with a trace of pride. "I did suggest this afternoon that the shirt could have been stolen from Harry, didn't I?"

"You did, my sweet. So I repeat, King: what if it was Harry's shirt we saw on somebody else?"

"A new perspective opens. Hypotheses present themselves. Egregious villains menace Harry Gardiner."

"Stop talking like Nero Wolfe. Say for the nonce that there is only one shirt like Harry's." He glanced across the room to where Harry Gardiner and Justin Lewis, his cousin and traveling companion, were sitting together, nibbling hors d'oeuvres and drinking short glasses of tonic water with no gin in it. "Why would anyone want to steal it?"

"It's a pretty shirt," Carol said. "I'd steal it myself if it were a dress."

They ignored her. "If it's genuinely a one-of-a-kind shirt, owned only by Harry Gardiner, then the only reason to steal it would be for purposes of identification—to make sure whoever wore that shirt would be identified as Harry Gardiner."

"But who could identify a strange drunk in Bububu as Harry Gardiner? Even if they wanted to?"

"Maybe us," Danforth said thoughtfully. "After all, we nearly did."

"We did," Helen said. "Not you. You had to ring in an old tattoo to spoil the scandal."

Leroy shook his head. "How would anybody know we were going to Bububu? We decided to do it on the spur of the moment. How could they be sure we'd recognize the shirt as Harry's? How could they expect to fool us with a transparent masquerade like that when we know Harry in the flesh? And know that he never touches a drop of the stuff."

Danforth rubbed a big hand over his crewcut and grinned at his partner. "If the man in that shirt was supposed to be Harry, then old Harry was also supposed to look gloriously stoned. But to whom?"

"There was another car behind the hotel," Leroy reminded them.

"Belonged to the drunk. Or the bartender."

"Maybe not. Maybe a third party was present."

"Hiding?"

"Hiding in a grove of clove," Helen laughed. "There's a song title for you."

"Wait! Danforth's stupendous brain is at work," King said immodestly. "How's this? The bad guy in this drama, whoever he is, set up the drunk scene with Harry's shirt not for our eyes, nor for anyone's—but for the keen impersonal eye of the camera!"

"Hear, hear!" his wife said.

"I'd like another gimlet," Helen said.

"King's right." Leroy waved to the bar steward. "Didn't you girls immediately jump to the conclusion that it was Harry you saw in King's picture?"

"True."

"So maybe the bad guy wasn't finished with the setup when we interrupted him. He hid from us. But after we left, he might have taken another picture of the drunk with all the little inconsistencies like the tattoo not showing—a picture that would say 'Harry Gardiner' to everyone who saw it and knew Harry. And it would say not only 'Harry Gardiner' but also that 'Harry Gardiner is as tight as a tick!' " Leroy laughed. "How about that?"

"Delicious," Carol acknowledged, tasting her fresh drink.

"If you young men will listen to a word of advice from a jaded old woman," Helen interposed, "there is a very simple way to stop all this speculation and have our dinner in peace. I hate to point out the obvious."

"Ask Harry about his shirt?" Leroy smiled at her.

"Exactly. Just ask him if somebody stole his shirt."

"Okay." Leroy arose. "Don't let anybody steal my drink."

He walked over to Harry Gardiner's table. For a few moments they could see him chatting animatedly with Harry and his cousin, Justin Lewis. Then he came back and sat down, somewhat glumly.

"The shirt was in Harry's drawer, clean, when he dressed for dinner tonight at six. Harry spent all afternoon at a Hindu dentist's, ashore. Justin was with him. The name Bububu meant nothing to either of them, as far as I could tell. End of report."

"So let's eat," Danforth said. "We can't win 'em all, pal. Finish your drink."

They went down to dinner.

* * * *

Halfway through his roast ptarmigan leg and asparagus tips, Leroy suddenly arrested his fork in midair, fixed his eyes sternly on his wife, and said, "The shirt could have been laundered and returned to Harry's drawer before he came back from the dentist."

"Whoops!" Carol said. "Here we go again."

"We saw the shirt on the drunk at about three o'clock," Danforth said. "So there would have been time to get it back to the ship."

"Laundered?" asked Helen skeptically. "Washed and dried and ironed—all in an hour or so?"

"Why not? Somebody who has the run of the ship could easily have done it in the ship's laundry."

"But who?"

Leroy said, "The 'who' might become evident if we knew the 'why.' Why would anybody go to all that trouble? Steal Harry's shirt, put it on a drunken bum in Bububu, take a photograph, then rush back here and get the shirt laundered and returned to Harry's stateroom before Harry got back on board?"

"Because they didn't want Harry to know about it," Carol said.

"I marvel at your deductive powers," King graciously allowed, "but I submit that you answered only the last, and the simplest, part of the question."

Leroy held up his hand for attention. He was peering across the dining room. Beyond the central smorgasbord table, they could see Harry Gardiner and his cousin at their table for two. Harry was reaching under the table to retrieve his napkin from the floor, his cheek almost touching the tabletop, his face distorted with the effort. At that moment a flash bulb flared as the ship's photographer, Jerry Nicholas, passed by, taking pictures, as usual, of various groups in the hope of selling souvenir prints to them.

Danforth followed Leroy's gaze. His eyes narrowed. "Who was Jerry photographing?" he asked Leroy. "Just then? That last flash?"

"Harry Gardiner," Leroy said. "As he is now? Groping under the table for his napkin?"

"Yes."

They watched the photographer laugh, say something to Harry Gardiner, then take another picture of the tablemates. Danforth grunted.

"What's got into you two?" Carol asked.

"Nothing," Leroy said softly. He finished his ptarmigan in silence. Only then did he murmur to his partner, "Was it deliberate, King? Just as Jerry approached?"

"It's a gag," Danforth replied, suddenly gay.

"And still none of our business."

"I'm finished," Carol announced. "Let's go up and play Bingo."

The next day, among the photographs Jerry Nicholas posted on the Promenade deck, Danforth and Leroy found a picture of Harry Gardiner and Justin Lewis sitting conventionally at their dining table. As expected, there was no picture of Harry groping under the table for his napkin.

Leroy said, "The way I see it, there are three possibilities. One, there's another shirt like Harry's and we saw it yesterday in Bububu. Two, the whole thing is rigged for a gag and there's no real harm in it. Three, it could be a build-up for a serious crime."

Danforth nodded. "I think we ought to talk to Harry. Just on the off-chance that it's for real, Mart."

"Me, too. He's a pleasant fellow, although rich."

"I'll find him and invite him for a cocktail before lunch," Danforth offered. "You warn the girls to let us handle all the talking."

* * * *

Harry Gardiner met them in the Viking Lounge, forward, deserted before luncheon except for them and a bartender. Harry ordered plain tonic water. They ordered their usual gimlets.

"This is very pleasant," Harry said, puzzled as to why they had invited him without his cousin.

Danforth began abruptly, "Harry, you know what we do for a living? We write mystery stories, Mart and I, and we're inveterately curious about anything that seems to contain even a hint of mystery. It's our business. So please try to understand and forgive us for what you will no doubt consider in extremely bad taste on our part. We want to ask you some questions. Personal questions."

"Fire away," Harry said agreeably. "I'm not sensitive. And you've got me curious, too."

With a sense of climax that made his hand tremble slightly, Danforth drew from his jacket pocket the Bububu snapshot. He handed it to Harry. "We took this in a village on Zanzibar Island yesterday," he said. "Is that your sports shirt?"

Harry looked. "It sure is. You told me yesterday you thought you'd seen one like mine. But this isn't like mine—it is mine. The only one there is."

"Do you recognize the man wearing the shirt, Harry? The drunk with the anchor and snake tattoo on his arm?"

"Never saw him before to my knowledge. It's hard to tell just from the top of his head."

Leroy took over. "Fine, Harry. We needed to know that. But we need to know something else even more. Why don't you ever take a drink?"

Carol and Helen winced at the bluntness of this question. Harry's face flushed; he dropped his eyes and hesitated before he replied, but they sensed no reservation in his answer.

"When I was younger, before my father died, I had a little trouble with liquor," he confessed in a low voice. "Hell, let's face it, I had big trouble with liquor. I was an alcoholic, or as near as made no difference. I was a great disappointment to my father. He never swallowed a drop in his life, although he was as tough and hard-bitten a wildcatter as any in Texas. For his sake, I finally managed to pull myself loose. I quit cold. Spent months in a sanitarium. And I haven't touched a drop since. I'm afraid to. That answer your question?"

"Yes." Danforth lit a cigarette. "Yes, it does. And thanks for being frank, Harry." He smoked silently for a few moments, then said, "You say your father was disappointed in you. How disappointed?"

"Plenty." Harry was emphatic. "Enough to make my continued sobriety a condition in his will." Leroy and Danforth let out their breath together.

"Ah," Leroy said. "Then a photograph purporting to show you dead drunk in a dive in Zanzibar wouldn't be considered exactly a good joke by the folks back home, would it?"

Harry Gardiner didn't even smile. "You're talking about the income from approximately three million bucks," he said, "to get grossly commercial about it. I get the income, or I don't get it, depending on my staying off the juice. That's how my father fixed it. So if a photo of me drunk were presented to my father's trustees, I could kiss my income goodbye. Provided it was a legitimate photograph, of course—recognizably me and indubitably drunk."

"A photo like that is exactly what somebody's planning to show your trustees, I'm afraid," Danforth said.

Harry laughed uneasily. "That snapshot of yours? It's not me—even if he is wearing my shirt. The tattoo gives it away, the face doesn't show—it's all wrong but the shirt. And where the hell they got my shirt—"

"There's such a thing as retouching a tattoo mark out of a picture," Danforth offered quietly. "And there's also such a thing as stripping your face into the negative of a different man's picture—so that even an expert can't tell whether it's a fake or not."

Harry digested this in silence. Finally he said skeptically, "It would take a professional photographer to do something like that."

"We have one on the ship," Leroy said.

"Jerry Nicholas? He's a nice kid. Why should he do such a thing? And where would he get a photograph of me that he could 'strip' into a setup like this?" He waved the Bububu snapshot in his hand.

Leroy told him about the picture that Nicholas had taken of Harry the night before—bending down groping for his napkin, his cheek almost on the tablecloth, his face twisted.

"Remember?" Leroy prodded. "Jerry took another shot after that one—the one that's on the board now. But the first one may have been what he really wanted. It would give him just the face he needed to strip into the picture he took of the drunk at Bububu yesterday. Proper positioning of your head to show your face clearly from the side—drunken expression—lying in a pool of spilled whiskey."

"My God!" Harry said, aghast. "You boys don't fool around, do you? Tell me this. Who would want to ruin me with a phony trick like that? Not Jerry Nicholas. He doesn't even know me, except to say hello." For a moment there was silence.

Carol and Helen finished their drinks and set their glasses down woodenly. Then Danforth said carefully, "It's possible that your cousin Justin got you into the proper position for Jerry to photograph last night. It's possible he deliberately brushed your napkin off your lap without your knowledge, then told you it was on the floor just as Jerry Nicholas approached your table with his camera."

Harry's eyes changed. "He did tell me I'd dropped my napkin."

"Which he couldn't have noticed unless he had engineered it," Leroy added.

"But Justin! He's my closest friend as well as my cousin. I take him on every one of my trips. He'd know damn well what such a picture would do to me."

"Let me ask one more question," Danforth said gently. "Who gets the income from your three million dollars if you forfeit it by hitting the bottle?"

They could hardly hear his answer, his voice was pitched so low. "It would be divided equally among my three cousins."

"Of whom Justin is one?"

"Of whom Justin is one." Harry shivered a little. "You're joking, aren't you? Just pulling my leg? This isn't on the level, is it?"

"We can find out pretty quick," Danforth said. "I left word that we'd like to see Jerry Nicholas here at twelve thirty."

The ship's photographer appeared a few moments later, carrying his Graflex. He came over to their table. "Hi," he said breezily, "Want a picture of this happy group?"

"No," Leroy said quietly. "We want to see the picture you made of Mr. Gardiner yesterday at Bububu."

Nicholas stopped smiling and stared. "What? I didn't take any picture of Mr. Gardiner at Bububu."

"That's right," Danforth said. "You didn't. The picture Mr. Leroy means is the one you took yesterday of that drunk at Bububu wearing Mr. Gardiner's sports shirt. And with the tattoo touched out. And the shot of Mr. Gardiner's face that you took last night substituted for the drunk's face—you know, Jerry, the gag shot you're building for Mr. Lewis."

For what seemed an eternity Jerry Nicholas continued to stare at them, wordless. Then he grinned disarmingly, shrugged his camera strap higher on his shoulder, and visibly relaxed.

"So you know about that," he said, "Mr. Lewis' gag birthday gift for you, Mr. Gardiner. Too bad. Mr. Lewis will be awfully disappointed you found out about it. He wanted it to be a surprise. He gave me a hundred bucks to rig it and make it look genuine. And he swore me to secrecy. I haven't told a soul. Who gave it away?"

Harry Gardiner swallowed hard. "These people figured it out," he said.

Nicholas nodded. "I was afraid they might recognize the shirt in Bububu yesterday on the waterfront drunk I hired to wear it for the trick shot."

"Where were you when we stopped there?" Leroy asked.

"Hiding in my car. I heard you coming and ducked. No time to hide the drunk though. He was already as stiff as a coot." Jerry sighed heavily. "All that work wasted! Even laundering that damn shirt. And my shot of you going after your napkin last night, Mr. Gardiner—it was beautiful, perfect. Oh, well."

In a grim voice Harry finally said, "You can keep the hundred bucks, Jerry. But I want all the negatives you took of this whole business—all the prints, too. It's not that I don't appreciate a sense of humor, but this gag doesn't seem very funny to me, not really. Shall we go to your office now?"

"Sure, Mr. Gardiner," Jerry said "It was just a gag. No offense,] hope?"

They left together. But not before Harry Gardiner turned to Danforth and Leroy and said simply, "Thanks. Thanks very much."

Danforth took a deep breath. "A-okay," he murmured to Leroy.

"All systems 'go'," his partner nodded. Gravely they shook hands with each other, as much in relief as in triumph.

Carol, her imposed silence ended at last, called loudly to the bar steward for another round of gimlets.

And Helen, rising a few moments later with a drink in her hand, paraded solemnly around the table and chanted an extemporaneous paean of praise:

"If you have dirty work to do.
Stay far away from Bububu.
For villainy cannot get far
When Leroy King's in Zanzibar!"

The Japanese Card Mystery

The cruise ship *Valhalla* moved sedately across a moon-washed quiet Pacific toward Japan. Aboard her, King Danforth and Martin Leroy were having a nightcap in the Horseshoe Bar when their wives, who had been playing bridge in the card room, joined them.

Danforth noted at once that his wife's dark eyes were glinting with excitement. He said, "You and Mr. Sakaguchi must have won again, Carol."

"Did they ever!" Helen Leroy said. "They beat Miss Wilkins and me three-straight rubbers as easily as if they could see every card in our hands."

"Sakaguchi wouldn't peek," Leroy said judiciously. "That honorable Japanese gentleman is far above cheating at cards."

"You're quite right there," Carol agreed. "And besides, he has much better card sense than you have, King."

"My card sense is impeccable," Danforth stated with dignity. "I happen not to like bridge, that's all."

"I'm glad somebody finally mentioned card sense," Helen said, "because while Mr. Sakaguchi's is quite well developed, it definitely isn't in the same league with his niece's."

Leroy said, "His niece's?"

"Yes. She lives in Tokyo."

"And has this extra special card sense?" Danforth said.

"Exactly. So special it's mysterious."

"If it's a mystery, you have approached the right oracles." Leroy ostentatiously polished his fingernails on his lapel.

"Aren't you going to offer us a nightcap?" his wife asked.

"Certainly. If that's your price for the story."

"It is. I'll have a Grasshopper."

"Me, too," said Carol.

Leroy shuddered. "How you can drink that stuff is mystery enough for me," he muttered. "Two Grasshoppers here," he said to the bar steward.

"You won't believe this," Carol said. "It's wild."

Danforth grinned. "We've told some pretty wild ones ourselves." Under the collaboration name of "Leroy King" he and Martin Leroy had written more than 50 mystery books of which over 80,000,000 copies, in every language except Chinese and Russian, had been sold throughout the world. "So try us."

"Well, then," Carol began, "as we said, Mr. Sakaguchi and I beat Helen and Mrs. Wilkins quite easily. After three rubbers we stopped playing and just sat around exchanging idle conversation. Helen mentioned something about card sense. And that's when Mr. Sakaguchi smiled that darling smile of his that shows his gold tooth in front, and told us he had a niece in Tokyo who really had card sense. He wished we could meet her."

The Grasshoppers came. While Carol tested hers, Helen took up the story.

"I asked him what he meant by real card sense," she said, "and he solemnly informed us that if one of us picked a card out of the deck at random and called his niece on the telephone, she could tell us immediately which card we'd picked—just like magic."

"Over the telephone?" Leroy grunted. "That's not magic, that's some kind of con game. When he calls his niece, he simply gives her a signal indicating which card's been drawn."

Carol interrupted. "Oh, no," she said. "He doesn't make the call to his niece. You do. He doesn't speak to her at all—not one word. So how could he signal her?"

Helen giggled, then tried to conceal it by clearing her throat and brushing a strand of blonde hair out of one sapphire-blue eye.

"That's a guilty giggle," Leroy said suspiciously. He turned to his wife. "Did you actually telephone this niece of Sakaguchi's?"

Helen tossed her head. "We couldn't just let an unbelievable statement like that pass, could we?"

Danforth, stricken, said to Carol, "You mean you and Helen actually telephoned Tokyo? By radio telephone? From the middle of the Pacific Ocean?" They nodded brightly. Danforth groaned. "There go our royalties on *The India Relish Mystery*, Mart! (Editors' Note: One of the series of novels about culinary crimes that include *The Danish Pastry Mystery*, *The London Broil Mystery*, and *The Bermuda Onion Mystery*.) What they charge you to use that radio telephone is murder!" Abruptly he asked his wife, "Did Sakaguchi's niece guess the right card?"

"How could she?" Leroy scoffed. "A thousand miles away and over the telephone!"

But Helen and Carol solemnly lifted their right hands and crossed their hearts. "We swear she did," Helen said. "The six of diamonds."

"Wait a minute." Danforth shook his crew cut head. "That's impossible. Unless Sakaguchi picked out the card from the deck, right? Maybe he's a cardsharp—can cut any card he wants to, for example—or his niece had foreknowledge of it..."

His voice trailed off as he saw both Helen and Carol shaking their heads. "Good try, buster," Carol sympathized, "but no cigar for you. I picked out the card. Mr. Sakaguchi didn't even touch the deck."

Leroy said, "It has to be a trick. Long-distance card sense is nonsense, to coin a *bon mot*."

Helen gave him a sweet smile. "Mr. Sakaguchi says his niece's senses, all of them, are finely tuned, unnaturally sharp, including her hearing. She can detect in the human voice, even over the telephone, all sorts of revealing vibrations and informative nuances that tell her infallibly exactly which card you've just drawn."

"I'll bet," said Leroy with open skepticism.

Carol laughed. "That's just what we tried to do. I told Mr. Sakaguchi I didn't believe it and offered to bet him on it."

"How much?" asked Danforth in mock alarm, that was not so mock.

"A dollar."

"Not even enough to pay for the telephone call," Danforth said bitterly, "even if you'd won. But there it is, Mart. A bet. It's a con game for sure."

"Oh, no," Carol said, "because Mr. Sakaguchi wouldn't bet with me. Or with Helen or Mrs. Wilkins, either. We all offered to bet."

"A dollar! No wonder he wouldn't bet!"

Helen offered in an off-hand manner, "Mrs. Wilkins is loaded, did you know that? Her husband left her six department stores and a chain of groceries. She offered to bet Mr. Sakaguchi five thousand dollars."

Leroy whistled. Danforth whispered as though in pain, "Five grand!"

Carol said, "Mr. Sakaguchi wouldn't think of exploiting his niece's clairvoyance or clairhearance, or whatever it is. But since we seemed interested, he insisted that we prove his niece's ability for ourselves, and let him pay for the phone call."

"And then, from the informative vibrations of your dulcet voice," Leroy sneered, "Mr. Sakaguchi's niece divined the six of diamonds?"

"She certainly did."

"If you'll pardon a vulgarity," Danforth said, "nuts!"

The girls drained their Grasshoppers in triumph and licked the last drops of liquor from the glasses' rims. "That's how it happened, fellows," Helen said smugly, "and since you're so notoriously expert at solving mysteries, be our guests!"

Leroy scratched his head and said gloomily, "Tell us more about the telephone call."

"We cut the cards first in the card room," Helen volunteered. "I shuffled the deck a couple of times and Carol cut the six of diamonds and showed it to us. Then we all went up to the radio room together and Carol placed the call with Mr. Holm, the radio operator."

"To what number in Tokyo?" Leroy asked.

"Heavens, I don't remember," Carol said. "Mr. Sakaguchi told Mr. Holm the number."

"Aha?" said Danforth with a glance at Leroy.

"No 'aha' about it," Helen objected. "Mr. Sakaguchi made no secret of the number. He called it out loud and clear, but who remembers telephone numbers, especially Japanese ones?"

"Not you, anyway," Danforth conceded. "Continue."

"It's a clear night," Carol went on, "not a bit of static, so Mr. Holm got the call through quickly, maybe in ten minutes. While we were waiting, Mr. Sakaguchi told us his niece speaks English—he wrote down her name for us on a cablegram blank, and told us how to pronounce it. When the call came through, I took it."

"And what exactly did you say?"

"I said 'Hello.' And a sexy-sounding female voice said 'Hello' right back at me. I said, 'Is this Myanoshima Hakkaido?—that's her name—and she said, 'Yes, who is calling, please?' She had a little trouble with her l's but her English was quite good."

"Then what? Give us every detail."

"Then I told her who I was and that her Uncle Sakaguchi claimed she could tell me what playing card I had just drawn from the deck. She laughed and said, 'He is such a nuisance, my dear uncle! Was it the six of diamonds?' and hung up."

There was a respectful silence when she finished. Finally Danforth breathed, "Beautiful!"

"What's that supposed to mean?" Helen asked.

"I know how it was worked, that's all."

"You don't!"

"Oh, yes," Leroy cut in. "Two possible ways. First, the telephone number. Sakaguchi could have fifty-two telephone numbers lined up, a different one for each card in the deck, at each of which some girl—ostensibly his niece—is prepared to tell you what card you've drawn if she gets a call like yours, Carol. Sakaguchi merely had you call the six-of-diamond's number." He grinned. "A rudimentary system."

Before either of the girls could say anything, Danforth said, "The other possibility's more likely, I think. After all, fifty-two telephone numbers! And fifty-two 'nieces' to answer the phone! Remember, Sakaguchi apparently does this trick just for kicks, since he wouldn't accept Mrs. Wilkins' bet. So why would he go to all that trouble and expense, just to play a practical joke?"

"He wouldn't," Helen decided firmly. "What's your other possibility?"

Danforth said, "The niece's name. Right, Mart?"

"Head of the class," Leroy proclaimed.

"What about her name?" Helen demanded.

"Well, listen," Danforth explained. "Everybody who telephones a stranger invariably begins by asking 'Is this Joe Smith' or 'Is this Suzy Brown,' or whatever, don't they? All right, now suppose the name Smith is the code word for Clubs; let's say Brown is the code name for Diamonds; Gardner means Hearts; and Miller denotes Spades. In addition, there are thirteen code first names like Joe and Suzy, each one meaning a number, to go with the four last names. The person called has a list of those code names beside her telephone. So somebody calls up and says, 'Is this Joe Smith? Can you tell me what card I've drawn?' All the 'niece' has to do is look down her list of code names till she finds Joe which means six, and Smith, which means

Diamonds. So she knows right away the card picked is the six of diamonds. She was tipped off by the full name you've called. Get it? Simple as ABC. The name you've called is the code name Sakaguchi has told you to call. Right?"

Carol said, "Do you mean that when I asked for Myanoshima Hakkaido tonight on the telephone I was really saying 'six of diamonds'?"

"Sure," Leroy said. "If your card had been the deuce of spades, Sakaguchi might have told you his niece's name was Kaori Fujiyama, or something."

Carol and Helen stood up. "You two geniuses take all the joy out of life!" Helen murmured. "Here we had a good mystery going, and you've punctured it like a toy balloon. Oh, well, let's go to bed, shall we?"

Carol yawned. "Let's. But I'm not convinced. I still think Mr. Sakaguchi's niece has long-distance card sense. She had such a lovely voice."

With which crashing non-sequitur she swept out of the bar.

* * * *

At noon the next day Danforth and Leroy were fifteen minutes late joining their wives for their regular pre-luncheon Gimlets.

"Where in the world have you been?" Helen asked. "Down at the pool, watching that overblown Mrs. Jocelyn in her bikini again?"

"No," answered her husband with a chastened air. "We've been telephoning Mr. Sakaguchi's niece in Tokyo."

"What!"

"Yes. We braced Mr. Sakaguchi and begged him to let us try—purely out of professional interest—his niece's extra-sensory perception."

"And what happened?"

"I cut the nine of hearts," Danforth said. "We called the Tokyo number. It was the same number you called last night, incidentally, according to Mr. Holm. I talked to the niece. And you're right—she has a very sexy voice." He paused. "And furthermore, she guessed the nine of hearts quicker than I could say Sakaguchi!"

Leroy grinned. "And guess what Mr. Sakaguchi told us his niece's name was this time?"

"What?" asked Carol and Helen together.

"Myanoshima Hakkaido," Danforth said dismally. "The same name he told you!"

* * * *

By cocktail time the story was all over the ship.

Carol and Helen couldn't resist the temptation to tease their husbands in front of assorted witnesses about their signal failure to solve such a simple mystery. Scores of passengers begged Mr. Sakaguchi to let them cut a card and test his niece's amazing powers by radio telephone. Scores of scoffers offered to wager him on the outcome.

Smiling his gold-toothed smile, Mr. Sakaguchi steadfastly refused, saying he couldn't permit his niece to be further harassed as the result of an innocent but thoughtless boast on his part. He refused to tell anyone the niece's telephone number; so, also, did the Danforths, Leroys, and Mr. Holm, the radio man, in spite of the numerous requests for it. Mr. Sakaguchi had asked them to keep it to themselves out of consideration for his niece's privacy.

As for Danforth and Leroy, they maintained a detached, preoccupied air that their wives readily recognized as their "plot conference" mood. Their failure to solve the mystery was obviously rankling; but they did not begrudge Mr. Sakaguchi his little joke.

Until two nights later, when the shattering news ran through the ship that Mr. Sakaguchi had won $50,000 from Mr. Starbuck, a wealthy, loud, and generally disliked passenger, who had bet him that amount that his niece couldn't guess a card which he drew from the deck.

Then Leroy said, "Just as we thought. A con game. Sakaguchi's been waiting for a really big sucker, that's all. Long-distance card sense! That's a laugh!"

Helen ventured, "You were talking only yesterday about authenticated cases of mental telepathy between Australian bushmen a thousand miles apart."

"But not over the telephone!" Danforth said. "Sakaguchi has a gimmick—he's got to have!"

"What he's got," Carol said with spirit, "is a niece with long-distance card sense, that's what I think. And that's what I'll keep on thinking until you prove I'm wrong."

"At the risk of repeating myself," said Danforth, "nuts!"

* * * *

Before their wives were up the next morning, Danforth and Leroy met at the shuffleboard court on the Sports Deck for their regular early morning game. But they did not play. Leroy took an envelope from his pocket.

"It came to me in the night," he said. "Look. I've written down the niece's name and broken it up into what sound like syllables when you say it. See if anything strikes you, King."

He had printed the name My-an-o-shi-ma Ha-ka-i-do on the back of the envelope.

Danforth looked at it and presently nodded. "Four syllables in the last name," he said. "And four suits in a deck of cards. That what you mean?"

"Precisely."

"So it's in the pronunciation, eh?"

"Sure. What American, unfamiliar with Japanese words and names, would know, recognize, or remember the proper way to pronounce a complicated name like Myanoshima Hakkaido? If Sakaguchi tells one of us his niece's name is Hak-ka-I-do with the emphasis on the i, and later tells somebody else it's HAK-ka-i-do, with the emphasis on the Hak, who's to notice the difference if he says it fast and fluently?—as he does. All we do is pronounce the name as nearly as we can."

"So," said Danforth, "we can reasonably conclude that if you say over the telephone to Sakaguchi's niece, 'Is this Miss HAK-ka-i-do' it means, say, Clubs; if you ask for Hak-KA-i-do, it means Diamonds; Hak-ka-I-do means Hearts; and Hak-ka-i-DO means Spades. For the life of me, I can't remember exactly how Sakaguchi told us to pronounce it." He shrugged. "So I guess variations in syllable emphasis wouldn't be noticed, as you say."

Danforth continued to look at the printed name. "How about this first name, though?" he asked then. "Only five syllables, and we need thirteen variations to cover all the cards."

"That," said Leroy, "is what I hoped you'd be able to figure out."

"Give me your envelope and a pen," Danforth said. Rapidly he jotted down this list:

Ace...MEE-an-o-shi-ma
2 ...Mee-AN-o-shi-ma
3   Mee-an-O-shi-ma
4 ...Mee-an-o-SHI-ma
5... Mee-an-o-shi-MA
6... MY-an-o-shi-ma
7... My-AN-o-shi-ma
8... My-an-O-shi-ma
9... My-an-o-SHI-ma
10 ...My-an-o-shi-MA
Jack...?
Queen...?
King...?

He showed it to Leroy. "How about this?" he queried. "Changing the pronunciation of the first, syllable from My to Me would give us ten of the thirteen variations we need."

"But why pick on the y for a change in pronunciation?"

"Because I have a hunch it's usually pronounced ee. Think of Hiroshima, Hirohito, Fujiyama, Nagasaki. But I'm almost sure Sakaguchi pronounced it eye when he told us his niece's name. He kind of slurred it, but it was more my than me. That's how Carol said it, too. That's why I think maybe her six of diamonds was MY-an-o-shi-ma, and my nine of hearts was My-an-o-SHI-ma."

"Not impossible. In fact, quite likely. But what about the Jack, Queen, and King? They're still missing."

Danforth sighed. "How right." Then he stared at his partner. "What did you say just then?"

"I said the Jack, Queen, and King are still missing."

Danforth laughed. "That's it!" he cried. "Miss! Listen, Mart, what word would be a perfectly natural one to add to the question 'Is this Myanoshima Hakkaido'?"

Leroy nodded. "Miss Myanoshima Hakkaido. Just add the word Miss in front of the proper pronunciation of Myanoshima for, say, the ace, deuce, and trey—and you tip off the Jack, Queen, and King?"

"It could be. Or even Mrs. or Mr. for that matter."

Leroy shook his head. "Not with that sexy female voice you raved about. It's got to be Miss." He thought for a moment. "Let's talk to the clever Mr. Sakaguchi without the girls being present, shall we? We may be wrong again, and I don't want to repeat the humiliation of being laughed at by our own wives. Do you?"

"Definitely not. Where'll we talk to him?"

"My cabin, at ten thirty? The girls will be in the beauty shop."

Mr. Sakaguchi accompanied them to Leroy's cabin willingly and smilingly.

Danforth opened proceedings. "Mr. Sakaguchi," he said, "that fifty thousand dollars you won last night—"

"Yes?" Mr. Sakaguchi hissed a little on his s's.

"We were astonished that after refusing so many wagers on your niece's card sense, you finally yielded—and bet such a huge sum."

"It was a large bet, wasn't it?" Sakaguchi's smile tightened, his gold tooth winking. "But I was practically forced into it, you realize. To vindicate my niece, myself—and, ah, you and your wives as well." He was bland. "Mr. Starbuck intimated loudly and publicly that you and your charming ladies were my accomplices, in on my trick, deliberately helping me to perpetrate it out of a twisted sense of humor, or a desire to test out a crime plot."

Leroy crossed one knee over the other and swung his foot. "Well, we still think, Mr. Sakaguchi, that it is a trick. And I'll tell you something else we think. We think you deliberately used our wives and us as a convenient and respectable means of spreading the news about your niece's so-called card sense to everybody on this ship, thus arousing general interest in her ESP or telepathic powers. It was part of a calculated build-up that enabled you to win fifty thousand dollars last night."

Mr. Sakaguchi looked pained.

Danforth said, "It was very ingenious of you to challenge us, through our wives, to try to discredit your trick. That way you got it reported all over the ship that even Leroy King, professional mystery solvers, admitted defeat. That was the charming fillip, the attractively piquant bait you needed to bring out the really serious skeptics, the rich and eager scoffers, the self-confident, debunkers and big bettors like Mr. Starbuck. The kind of sucker who would relish being able to tell his chums later, why, he even fooled that well-known team of mystery writers, Leroy King, but he couldn't fool me!"

"You make me out cleverer than I am," Mr. Sakaguchi said. Without hesitation he went on smoothly, "If my niece's ability is a trick, perhaps you can demonstrate how it was done?"

"Maybe not exactly," Danforth said, "but we can show you how it could have been done."

Sakaguchi smiled. "I am fascinated," he said. "Please proceed."

Danforth went over to the bedside stand and got a deck of cards. "Mr. Leroy," he said, grinning in spite of himself, "will pretend to be your niece. And I shall be a credulous cruise passenger. We'll have to dispense with the telephone, but my partner will go into the bathroom where he cannot see which card I draw. Will that be satisfactory?"

"Eminently fair."

Leroy went into the bathroom and closed the door, leaving only a crack wide enough to hear through. Once inside, he pulled from his pocket a penciled list. "Go ahead," he called to Danforth.

Danforth, outside in the cabin, cut the deck of cards a few times, then showed the card he drew to Mr. Sakaguchi. The three of spades. After consulting a list of his own, he then called out to Leroy in the bathroom, "Is this Mee-an-O-shi-ma Hak-ka-i-DO? What card have I drawn?"

Leroy's voice promptly replied, "The three of spades."

Mr. Sakaguchi's face was expressionless. "Remarkable," he murmured.

Danforth cut the deck again, a few more times, then showed his card to Sakaguchi. "Is this My-an-o-SHI-ma Hak-ka-I-do? What card have I drawn?" he called to Leroy.

"The nine of hearts."

"Very interesting," Sakaguchi conceded. "May I draw a card myself?" At Danforth's nod, the Japanese leaned forward, cut, and smiled. He held out the King of Hearts. "I rather doubt that your partner can guess this one," he said.

"Is Miss Mee-an-O-shi-ma Hak-ka-I-do?" Danforth called out.

"No," came Leroy's muffled voice, "but the King of Hearts is here. Will that do?" With these words he opened the bathroom door and emerged.

"It will do very nicely," Mr. Sakaguchi said. "I congratulate you, gentlemen."

"Thanks," said Leroy. "I wish we could say the same. But since you have won fifty thousand dollars by fraud, from a compatriot of ours, using us as unknowing confederates, I believe our next step is clearly indicated: to expose you immediately to the captain of this ship and to our fellow passengers as a cheat, a confidence man."

"Please," said Sakaguchi. He spread his hands in a typical Oriental gesture. "I much prefer to call myself a fund raiser. It is a more truly descriptive term."

Danforth said, "You're a fund raiser, I'll hand you that."

"Only once a year, however," Sakaguchi said, "and in a very good cause." He took out his wallet and pulled from it a check. "Perhaps you would examine this check which Mr. Starbuck wrote me last night?"

Puzzled, Leroy said, "It isn't drawn to you or to your niece. It's made out to The Tokyo Home for Crippled Children."

Sakaguchi beamed. "Exactly," he said. "My favorite charity. My niece, Miss Myanoshima Hakkaido of recent fame, is the Directress of this Home. It is an expensive Home to operate properly, you can understand that. And many Japanese are notoriously chary of giving large charitable donations. So once a year, gentlemen, I conspire with my niece to raise fifty thousand dollars from some unpleasant tourist who is so wealthy he will not miss the money, but whose largess will substantially aid my niece in operating her Crippled Children's Home for another year."

He looked from Danforth to Leroy. "I confessed as much to Mr. Starbuck last night when he paid his bet. Also, I pointed out that he could deduct the full amount on his United States income tax return as a legitimate charitable contribution. He shook hands with me graciously enough—after telephoning a Tokyo lawyer he knows to confirm the existence of the Home, its Directress' name, and its telephone number."

"Well," said Danforth and Leroy, both dazed.

"Mr. Starbuck," Sakaguchi pressed on eagerly, "is willing to forget the entire incident. Can't you do the same? You've lost nothing. On the contrary, you gained the satisfaction of having solved a mystery that has baffled everyone exposed to it save yourselves." He paused. "I'm leaving the ship tomorrow, when we dock at Yokohama. I'm not finishing the cruise. And I would like to think you bear me no ill will for serving charity's sweet cause by using you and your charming wives as shills." He bared his gold tooth in a pleading smile.

Danforth and Leroy returned the grin. "It was our pleasure," Danforth said, bowing. "A privilege to help the Crippled Children's Home. But would you feel offended, Mr. Sakaguchi, if we just check a couple of things with Mr. Starbuck before you leave us tomorrow?"

The New Zealand Bird Mystery

An hour after the cruise ship *Valhalla* had left her berth at Queen's Pier in Hobart, Tasmania, and was nosing bravely into a choppy Tasman Sea en route to Wellington, New Zealand, everybody aboard knew that something terrible had happened to Homer Rice.

At first nobody knew exactly what, but shipboard gossip being what it is, everybody felt sure it was something terrible. For as the *Valhalla* pointed her trim bow eastward, and her passengers, wearied by a day and a half of strenuous sightseeing in Tasmania, settled down for their before-luncheon drinks, Homer Rice was nowhere to be found.

His friends, of whom there were many, sought him in his expensive cabin on the sundeck and then through the bars, public rooms, and various decks of the Norwegian liner, but with notable lack of success. Soon it developed that nobody had seen hide or hair of Homer Rice since he went ashore with the other passengers the previous morning, ostensibly to do the Hobart city tour, ascend Mt. Wellington by car, and visit briefly the apple orchards of the Huon River Valley.

Immediately rumors and counter-rumors began to fly through the ship as thick as fireflies in a summer dusk: Homer Rice was desperately ill in the ship's hospital, felled by a Tasmanian virus of unbelievable virulence; Homer Rice had left the cruise to fly home to California because his wife had suffered a stroke; Homer Rice had been jailed by Hobart police as a dangerous sex deviate because he had been seen buying a bag of caramel kisses for a small girl in a sweet shop.

The most distressing rumor originated from a busboy in the Chief Steward's department whose bunk was near the forward freezer in the bowels of the ship. From this lad came the shocking word that Homer Rice was not sick, had not departed for home by air, was not in jail, but was, in fact, dead. Otherwise, why had one of the empty caskets (which were discreetly carried below decks by the *Valhalla* on every extended cruise to accommodate passengers who failed to survive three months at sea)—why had one of these caskets, asked the busboy, been removed from the hold last night and stowed instead, with its lid decently closed, in the forward freezer room where he, personally, had seen it this morning?

This was a good question, as the Danforths and Leroys, sipping gimlets in the Horseshoe Bar, readily admitted. And Helen Leroy, who was always an exponent of direct action, reached up and caught the arm of the ship's doctor who happened to be passing their table, and turned her seraphic, irresistible smile on him.

"Doctor Hagen," she said, "everybody is saying that something awful's happened to Mr. Rice. Do you know anything about it?"

Dr. Hagen, tall, blond, and smoking a cigarette in a long black holder stuffed with filters, nodded courteously. "I am sorry to say it is true, Mrs. Leroy. The Captain will be making the announcement in a few minutes when he comes down from the bridge for luncheon. Mr. Rice is dead."

Carol Danforth put down her drink. "Oh, dear!" she said. "How terrible! Was he taken suddenly ill, Doctor?"

"No," said the doctor gravely. He knew the special interest of these four passengers in criminous matters. "Mr. Rice was not taken ill. He was killed."

"What!" King Danforth and Martin Leroy, better known as "Leroy King," the collaborating team that had authored scores of mystery novels, straightened in their chairs as though jerked by a single string. "Killed?" asked Danforth incredulously. "You mean murdered?"

The doctor leaned down closer to the table and lowered his voice. "Actually, a Hobart boatman stumbled over Mr. Rice about midnight last night, lying in the shadow of an apple warehouse along Constitution Dock. The boatman called the police. And the police, when they learned from his passport that Mr. Rice was a *Valhalla* passenger, notified Captain Thorsen, who called me when they brought Mr. Rice's body aboard in the middle of the night. He was already dead, unfortunately—there was nothing I could do for him."

"How was he killed?" Leroy asked.

"A blow on the head. His skull was smashed in."

Helen and Carol stared at the doctor, horror-stricken.

Danforth spoke up. "Was he robbed?"

The doctor nodded. "His wallet was missing. The Hobart police are looking at this moment for the robber. But please, say nothing of this to the other passengers, eh? It is not nice for a cruise to have a passenger killed. The Captain will announce merely that Mr. Rice died suddenly. He was not in good health, you know."

The doctor moved on. Danforth stared out of the window beside him at the blowing whitecaps that topped the uneasy sea through which the *Valhalla* labored, and he muttered under his breath, "Murdered! Poor Homer!"

Leroy glanced at his watch. "Drink up, girls," he said in a preoccupied way, "It's time for lunch."

Helen pushed away her half-empty glass. "I don't feel like drinking," she said. "I liked Homer Rice!"

Everybody had liked Homer Rice—the quiet, intelligent, unassuming timber company executive who had been traveling around the world on the *Valhalla* for his health. So when Captain Thorsen made his brief announcement of Rice's death at luncheon, a pall of sincere regret, if not genuine grief, settled on Rice's former fellow passengers. And a renewed murmur of speculation burst forth at once over the luncheon tables.

Carol Danforth said indignantly, "I'll bet that ridiculous publicity we got in Tasmania yesterday was responsible for Homer Rice's death!"

"What publicity?" asked her husband.

"You didn't see it? The article in the Hobart newspaper yesterday morning? With the headline 'Shipload of American Millionaires Visits City'? Whoever killed Homer Rice probably thought he'd be carrying his million in his wallet."

Danforth said, "I don't agree. Surely everybody in the world, including Tasmanians, must know that all Americans—and especially traveling Americans—live strictly on credit cards and travelers checks. Why, cash is positively indecent today."

"You know what I mean," said Carol indignantly. "That newspaper story could have misled some dumb thug into thinking we all carry oodles of cash with us—and poor Homer Rice was killed as a result. Isn't that possible?"

"Sure," said Leroy. "And selecting Homer as the victim could also have been purely accidental."

Helen put up a hand to her blonde hair. "Do we have to discuss it? It's ghoulish to hash it over like one of your mystery plots, Martin."

Her husband patted her hand. "You must admit that Carol has raised an interesting point, Helen." He looked a trifle guiltily at his partner.

Danforth took the cue. "I could stand to know how much cash Homer actually was carrying in his wallet when he was killed," he said.

"Now, King!" said Carol. "Stop it!"

Danforth grinned at his dark-haired vivacious wife. "Only way to prove conclusively that Homer was just an accidental victim," he murmured with a deprecatory air. "No large amount of cash on him, no reason for anybody to rob him in particular. And vice versa, if you see what I mean."

Carol cut into her strawberry torte dessert. "You would look for plot material in the natural death by old age of your own grandmothers!" she said. "Why don't we just forget it?"

So they finished their luncheon in silence. When they rose from the table and started out of the dining room, Danforth nudged Leroy, then said blandly, "We'll meet you in ten minutes at our deck chairs, girls."

"Where are you going?" asked Carol suspiciously.

"Little errand. It's indelicate of you to ask."

Carol sniffed, raising her dark brows at Helen as they entered the elevator together. Danforth and Leroy got off at A-deck. Their wives continued upward.

Within the promised ten minutes Danforth and Leroy rejoined the ladies in their secluded deck chairs on the sundeck. Homer Rice's chair, which had been only a few yards along the deck from theirs, was empty now. It looked forlorn.

Seeing the glint in her husband's eyes, Helen sighed and said, "Well, come on, out with it. Obviously you've got something to tell us."

Leroy said, "Homer Rice was probably carrying eight thousand five hundred dollars in cash when he was killed last night. What do you think of that?"

The girls stared. "How do you know?" asked Helen.

"The Purser told us just now," Danforth informed them. "He said he cashed eighty-five hundred dollars' worth of travelers checks for Homer between Sydney and Hobart, and Homer had never before cashed more than a hundred dollars at any one time. And there was no sign of the eighty-five hundred in Homer's cabin when the Hobart Police came aboard last night, the Purser says. So the chances are ten to one that Homer had the cash on him when he was killed."

In a small voice Carol said, "I suppose you've deduced

something of great significance from that, haven't you?"

"Why, yes," said Leroy, "we think we have."

"What?"

"That maybe Homer wasn't just a chance victim."

"But that would mean somebody knew beforehand he'd have all that cash on him," Helen objected.

"Exactly," her husband agreed. "The question is who."

"You're the experts," said Carol. "Who?"

Danforth shrugged. "The fellows in the Purser's office who saw him cash his travelers checks? The Purser himself? A passenger Homer confided in? Somebody who happened to note his bulging wallet, perhaps? There are a hundred possibilities."

"Rubbish!" declared Helen with spirit. "No passenger on this cruise, and none of those fellows in the Purser's office could be a thief and a murderer—not by any stretch of the imagination! And don't tell me they could!"

"Watch your grammar, sweetheart," said Leroy placidly. "We're not accusing anyone. But understandably, we can't resist speculating a little."

"Go ahead and speculate then," Carol smiled at Helen. "It's what we get for marrying a mystery writing team, Helen. Bear up, that's all we can do."

"And all we can do is speculate," said Danforth, "because as far as I can see, there's no possibility of getting a firm answer to the really important question."

"All right," Carol said, "I'll bite. What is the really important question?"

Danforth rubbed a hand over his crew cut head with a pleased look at his wife. "Viz," he answered, "to wit, i.e., e.g.: Why would Homer Rice, a legitimate millionaire whose credit is impeccable, suddenly need to get eighty-five hundred bucks worth of travelers checks cashed between Sydney, Australia, and Hobart, Tasmania?"

Broodingly Leroy said, "How about this, King? Homer was a West Coast lumber tycoon, right? And Tasmania,

I happen to know in my wisdom, is very big in timber. So maybe Homer had a big timber deal to settle in Hobart."

"If so, why not use the travelers checks themselves to seal the bargain? Or a cashier's check? Or a personal check, if it comes to that? Why cash?"

"M-m-m. And even more puzzling," said Leroy, lighting a cigarette, "is the latter half of your unanswerable question, King: why wait to get the cash until the last day before we arrived in Hobart? Homer was darned lucky the Purser's office had that much cash they could spare him, the Purser says."

Helen winked at Carol. "Perhaps," she suggested wickedly, "Leroy King isn't the world's best mystery team after all, Carol. Perhaps we've been overrating these husbands of ours. 'Unanswerable' questions, indeed!"

Her husband pretended deep hurt. "You will have to know this sometime," he said portentously, "so it may as well be now, girls. To be brutally frank, King and I married you for your beauty only, don't you realize that? Not for your brains. So do us a favor, will you? Just sit there in golden silence and look beautiful. And keep your sweet little traps shut when brilliant and mature men are discussing serious matters."

"Oh," said Helen, "you don't want me to answer your unanswerable question for you, is that it?"

Danforth and Leroy gazed somberly at her. "You can answer that question?"

"I can try."

"I withdraw my remark about your beauty," said Leroy, "and I apologize. You aren't beautiful at all. You're smart. So what's the answer?"

"It's perfectly obvious to ordinary, non-genius-type people like me," said Helen softly, "why Homer cashed all those travelers checks when he did. It was because he'd just learned he had to."

"That's a deceptively simple-sounding statement," said

Danforth. "But why the cash? And for what purpose? There's the rub."

Leroy looked thoughtful. "If Homer learned in Sydney that he'd need the cash for something in Hobart, and if the Sydney banks were closed when he learned it—"

Danforth growled, "That explains the timing, maybe. But that's all. Sure, Homer could have got a telephone call or a cable in Sydney telling him he'd need cash for some deal in Hobart—"

Leroy made an abrupt movement. "Or," he said, with sudden excitement in his voice, "a letter. A letter received in Sydney. Of course. I'll bet I saw him reading the very one!"

"You saw him? Where? When?" The others flung questions at him.

"Right there at the rail," Leroy pointed. "In front of his deck chair. He was standing with his back to me, reading a letter, a few minutes after we sailed from Sydney. He'd just got back aboard after a shore trip and had collected his mail in his cabin, I suppose."

Leroy closed his eyes, trying to recall details. "You three had collapsed in your bunks from weariness. I was sitting up here in my deck chair to see us sail out of Sydney Harbor, which, I might interject here, is commonly thought to be the most beautiful in the entire world. Homer was standing there at the rail, reading a letter. When he finished, he crumpled up letter and envelope together, I remember, and threw them over the rail. Then he turned around with a big happy grin on his face."

Leroy opened his eyes. "Wait," he said. Slowly he got to his feet and went a few yards along the deck toward Homer Rice's empty deck chair. He bent over the wooden grid that covered the shallow trough of the scuppers there at the foot of the rail. They saw him lift a yard-long section of scupper cover, pick something out of the dry trough below, then replace the grid.

He came back and sat down again. "Here it is," he said.

Helen gave him a worried look. "Here's what? Darling, let me see."

"The letter," Leroy said, "that Homer was reading." He opened his hand and showed them a crumpled ball of paper. "When he threw them overboard, I remember, the envelope and the letter separated, and the wind blew the letter back through the rail and into the scuppers. Homer didn't notice it, I guess. The envelope went on overboard."

In amazement Danforth said, "Total recall! Open the letter, Mart, and let's see what it says."

"Don't you dare," said Helen Leroy at once. "We have no right to read Homer's private correspondence, even if he's dead."

"This may tell us why he's dead," replied Leroy. He smoothed out the crumpled letter carefully.

It was an odd-looking letter—merely a scrap of heavy white paper, roughly triangular in shape, about four inches wide at the top, and with uneven edges indicating that it had been torn from a larger sheet. It was blank on one side; on the other side they saw both printing and calligraphy.

Two words in rather large type were printed in the upper left corner, parallel to the triangle's widest side: "logical jerk." And ten lines of spidery handwriting were underneath, necessarily compressed into shorter and shorter lines as the paper came to a point at the bottom.

logical jerk.
        At last. More than rumor this time.
     si. Confirmed Maori photo. Immed-
       iate need three ready for ex-
         pedition and live proof.
        Hobart, Aug. 12. Hon-
         orary degrees for
          both of us, I
         should think.
         Meanwhile,
          mum.

There was no signature.

Carol began to laugh.

"What's so funny?" demanded her husband.

"Poetic justice, that's what. Exactly what you deserve for reading other people's mail." Carol appealed to Helen. "How about that for a graphic two-word description of Leroy King, the deductive machine we married? 'Logical jerk'! It's perfect!"

She went off into fresh gales of merriment in which Helen now joined.

"We are not amused," Leroy said. Belying his words, he grinned broadly at his lanky partner who, surprisingly, was not smiling but gazing abstractedly at the ocean. Leroy recognized that far-off look. Danforth, it seemed, was in what Carol impishly referred to as "an old abandoned quandary."

Striving to penetrate Danforth's pre-occupation, Leroy continued, "This letter is pure gibberish—except for one thing."

Danforth failed to rise to the bait. Helen, however, ventured, "The 'Hobart, August twelfth' bit, you mean? That was yesterday, the day the *Valhalla* arrived in Tasmania, the day Homer Rice was killed and robbed."

"Good thinking," Leroy said. "So this crazy letter could have something to do with setting up Homer's rendezvous with death in Hobart. But if so, where's any mention of the cash Homer was supposed to bring ashore with him?" He glanced inquiringly at Danforth. "What do you think, King?"

Danforth roused himself from his reverie. "What? Think about what?"

"The fact there's no reference in this message to the eighty-five hundred in cash?"

Danforth rubbed his cropped head, then leaned over and reread the triangular letter in Leroy's hand. "Three," he said musingly. "Three. And mention of a Maori, which brings New Zealand to mind at once, since that's where

Maori natives live." He snapped his fingers. "Hey! What's the unit of money in New Zealand?"

"The pound," said Leroy.

"Worth how many dollars?"

"About the same as the English pound, I think. Two dollars and eighty cents, or thereabouts. Why?" Then Leroy got it. "Oh! Three thousand New Zealand pounds would come to about eighty-five hundred U.S. dollars, is that it?"

"Near enough," said Leroy. "It could be, especially if taken with the word 'ready' that follows the word 'three' in the message."

"By Jove!" said Leroy. "'Three ready.' Meaning three thousand pounds in ready cash?"

"Why not?" Danforth turned gloomy. "But the rest of this jazz about rumors and photos and honorary degrees is absolute Greek to me."

Leroy fixed his partner with a level look. "Why the brown study act just now?" he asked.

Danforth shrugged. "A nagger. A sneaky feeling I had that those two printed words, 'logical jerk,' rang a bell somehow. Somewhere recently I seem to have heard or seen those words. Or words very like them. But I can't think where."

Leroy looked at the two printed words at the top of the scrap of paper. "The word 'logical' is smack up against the left-hand margin of the paper," he said. "Maybe 'logical' isn't the complete word. Maybe the front part of the word was ripped off when the paper was torn out of wherever it came from."

Carol nodded. "Of course!" she said eagerly. "How about a physiological jerk, for instance? Or even a biological, zoological, ichthyological jerk?"

"What big words you use, Grandma," Leroy began when Danforth straightened up with one of Carol's physiological jerks.

"Hold it!" he cried. "That's it, by heaven! Carol, you're an intuitive catalyst!"

"Watch your language there, sailor," said Carol.

"The phrase I almost remembered," said Danforth slowly, "was 'ornithological jerk.' And now I know where we heard it."

"We heard it?" asked Helen doubtfully.

"Sure. We all did. It was in a verse that Campbell La Rue, our cruise lecturer, quoted several days ago in his informative talk to the passengers about New Zealand!"

"Talk about total recall," said Leroy, "you don't do badly yourself, old buddy. Now that you mention it, I remember it, too. A verse about a kiwi bird or some such, wasn't it?"

Helen chimed in, "A moa bird. I remember it now. Mr. La Rue said it came from a children's book of verses about Australian and New Zealand birds. It was cute."

Danforth stood up. "Pardon me," he said, "while I find Mr. La Rue."

"And Mr. La Rue's clue," added Helen. "Hurry back."

When Danforth returned to his deck chair a few minutes later, he brought with him a large square picture book whose title in yellow letters on a bright green cover could easily be deciphered while Danforth was still fifteen feet away. *Your Feathered Friends Down Under.*

"La Rue lent it to me," said Danforth, sitting down. Rapidly he leafed through pages of verses and colored illustrations dealing with emus, kiwis, cassowaries, kookaburras, keas, bellbirds, and many others. Only when he came to the last page in the book did he exclaim with satisfaction, "Ah! Here we are."

The page was headed "The Biggest Bird of All" and displayed a realistic drawing of an enormous ostrich-like moa bird. The accompanying text consisted of two stanzas in limerick form. Danforth read them aloud to his rapt audience.

> New Zealand, by some silly quirk
> Such as only Dame Nature can work,
> Gave birth, I have heard,

> To a bird so absurd
> 'Twas an ornithological jerk.
>
> For the moa, in New Zealand loa,
> Often grew to eleven foot foa.
> It was wingless and tame
> And it's really a shame
> That there aren't any moa any moa.

Leroy took the picture book from Danforth and examined the back of the last page. It was blank. The limericks were set in the same type and same size as the two printed words at the top of the letter. And between the first and second verses, below the words 'ornithological jerk,' there were several inches of white space.

Leroy superimposed Homer Rice's mysterious triangular letter on the book page, matching exactly the position of the two printed words, and it was immediately evident that whoever had written the odd note to the murdered man had cavalierly torn his writing paper out of the last page of a copy of *Your Feathered Friends Down Under*.

"But where does that get us?" asked Danforth at length. "Thousands of copies of this book must be kicking around. If only our lazy letter writer had thought to sign his name the way respectable people—"

"Excuse me," said Leroy suddenly, "for interrupting. But look at the name of the guy who wrote this bird book!"

"Eric Rhome," murmured Helen, puzzled.

Danforth crowed, "Well, how about that? Nothing escapes the X-ray eyes of Leroy King!"

"What's so special about the name Eric Rhome?" asked Carol plaintively. "Do you know him?"

"I think we did," said Danforth evenly. "Look. Just as 'Leroy King' is the pseudonym of the best mystery writers in the business, so Eric Rhome must have been the pseudonym of the man who wrote these children's verses about birds. For the name 'Eric,' with its letters arranged differently, spells 'Rice.' And the name 'Rhome,' ditto, spells

'Homer.' Do you see?"

"For heaven's sake!" exclaimed Helen. "Eric Rhome—Homer Rice! Then maybe it does mean something that this funny letter Homer got in Sydney was written on a scrap of paper torn from his own book?"

"Indubitably," said Leroy, his eyes shining now with the fervor of the incorrigible solver of puzzles. "Think of it. A timber tycoon in the eyes of the world, but a modest author of children's books in secret! And books about birds, yet!"

"Maybe he was a birdwatcher," Helen suggested. "Lots of men are."

"Birdwatcher or not, Homer was interested in birds and knew enough about them to write a book on the subject," interpolated Danforth, "if, as we think, he wrote this book. Australian and New Zealand birds, anyway. Can't we reasonably assume, therefore, that Homer had been to New Zealand and Australia before this trip?"

Leroy nodded vigorously. "Also that whoever wrote him this letter deliberately wrote it on a page fragment of Homer's book."

"Why?" asked Helen.

"To identify himself, perhaps. Remember the letter isn't signed. Maybe he was saying, 'This letter is from the guy who knows you wrote this book, Homer Rice.'"

"Why not sign his name?" This was Carol being irreverent again. "It would have been so much simpler."

"The letter says 'meanwhile, mum'," Leroy pointed out. "Everything very hush-hush. No names. Nothing but obscure hints."

Danforth said, "I've got another idea about identification."

"What?"

"Those two words in type—'logical jerk.' They might have been deliberately included for identification purposes, too."

"To identify that particular verse in the book, you mean?"

"Yes. And therefore, it follows, to identify a specific bird."

Leroy stared. So did Helen and Carol.

"A moa bird? The bird that was an ornithological jerk?"

"Why not?"

"I'll tell you why not," said Helen severely. "I happen to have a little of that total recall you're so proud of myself. And I remember that Mr. La Rue said in his lecture that the moa bird has been extinct for merely five hundred years, that's all. Just as the poem says, 'there aren't any moa any moa.' So why would anybody want to identify one in this letter?"

Leroy ignored her. "Do you mean, King," he asked with something approaching awe, "that you think the letter writer is writing about a moa bird?"

Danforth shrugged. "It sounds screwy. But why else would those two words in type be included in the letter? If you read the letter with a moa bird in mind, it begins to make sense, doesn't it? An impossible, incredible kind of sense, I'll admit, but sense anyway. Go on. Read the message again."

The three did so in silence. Then Carol said, "Do you seriously expect us to believe that whoever wrote this letter to Homer expected him to believe that somebody had discovered a live moa bird and actually taken a picture of it?"

"I don't know," said Danforth stubbornly. "But if you could come up with a live moa bird after they've been supposedly extinct for five hundred years, you'd be a pretty big man in birdwatching circles, wouldn't you? And in ornithological circles, too. And some university might even hand out honorary degrees to the men who were responsible for such an amazing scientific find, I should think."

"But—but—but—" stammered Helen. She sank back in her deck chair, stunned. "You're serious, aren't you, King?"

Danforth smiled at her. "Never more so, sweet."

"In that case," said Leroy, "this letter means that whoever wrote it is assuring Homer Rice that a Maori has actually seen and photographed a live moa bird, believed extinct, and needs three thousand pounds pronto to set up an expedition to go out and capture the live moa? That Rice was to meet him at Hobart yesterday with the money in cash? And if successful in proving that live moa birds still exist, both the letter writer and Homer Rice, who will finance the expedition, will probably win honorary degrees for their discovery?"

"Very succinctly put," said Danforth. "Don't you agree that it's a possibility?"

Carol challenged him. "Let me ask one small question. What's the Spanish word for 'yes' doing in this New Zealand letter? That little word 'si'? I suppose you deduce from that that the five moa birds have been discovered in Spain?" She sniffed in disdain.

Danforth looked sadly at his partner. Leroy said, "All women are notoriously skeptical of scientific truth." He turned to Carol. "Suppose," he said, "just for the sake of argument, that the word 'si,' instead of meaning 'yes' in Spanish, were interpreted as the initial letters of two very relevant New Zealand words?"

"What words?"

"South Island," returned Leroy. "The southernmost and largest island of the New Zealand group. The part of New Zealand where even recent maps still display the word 'Unexplored' over certain interior areas? What then?"

"I give up," said Helen. "Go ahead and dream."

Danforth obliged. "Let's say that Homer Rice is a birdwatcher or an amateur ornithologist. Somehow he's got the bee in his bonnet that moa birds are not extinct. On a previous trip or trips to New Zealand, he's been in touch with some local authorities about his theory. He's let it be known there that he's willing and eager to finance a search for live moa birds if there seems any chance they exist. But for Pete's sake, says Homer, keep the whole thing quiet until something definite can be proved, inasmuch as he doesn't want to become widely known as an insane birdwatcher. And evidently he's been in touch with the writer of this odd letter before, because the letter says 'more than rumor this time'—implying previous communication. How's that strike you?"

Leroy nodded. "And suppose our unknown New Zealand letter writer, a devious and dishonest birdwatcher if ever there was one, knew Homer Rice was taking this cruise for his health? And that the *Valhalla* would visit Hobart, Tasmania, on August twelfth? He writes to Homer in Sydney, dangling the carrot of a live moa before Homer's nose, and asks for the financing, as promised. Then, when Homer naively goes ashore with eighty-five hundred bucks in his jeans, this character is lurking on Constitution Dock, meets Homer, kills him, and calmly lifts the cash. Is that the picture you have?"

"Wait a minute," said Carol. "Why wouldn't the letter writer just have innocently met Homer in Hobart as proposed, and let him give him the money for the expedition as planned? That way, he'd get the money without violence or murder, and who's to blame him if the expedition never finds a moa bird?"

Leroy shook his head. "You're forgetting the photo mentioned in the letter. Homer was naive, maybe, but not a complete sucker. He'd want to see evidence—say, a photograph of a live moa bird—before he'd fork over the cash for an expedition."

"Then why did the letter writer mention the photo in the first place?"

"To convince Homer that this time it wasn't just a rumor, that he had proof of Homer's theory."

Danforth said, "He'd run almost no risk of being caught. His letter warns Homer to keep mum. He hasn't signed the letter. He sets up the murder rendezvous in Tasmania instead of in New Zealand where he lives. Just another rich American tourist robbed abroad, only unfortunately killed in the process. That's how he planned it."

"Whereas the truth is," said Leroy, "that a certain unscrupulous birdwatcher needed eighty-five hundred bucks and took the easiest way to get it—by playing on the credulity of an amateur American colleague who happened to be rich."

Danforth began to count on his fingers. "So what have we got? One, the murderer is somebody who lives in New Zealand. Two, he's probably somebody who is connected with ornithology or birdwatching. Three, the talk of honorary degrees suggests an academic orientation."

"Four," supplemented Leroy solemnly, "he's probably someone who is pressed for money. Five, he's somebody who has been in touch with Homer Rice before and knew the itinerary of this cruise and that Homer would be on it."

"Six," continued Danforth, "he's somebody who was absent from his usual haunts yesterday and probably part of today—flying to Tasmania from New Zealand, robbing Homer, and flying home again." He paused, "Anything else?"

Unexpectedly Carol Danforth said, "Let it never be said that I can't deduce along with the best. This letter written to Homer is triangular—shaped like a V. Could that mean the murderer's name begins with a V?"

"It could," said Danforth, "if more than one person in New Zealand knew that Homer wrote this bird book and some identification besides the page fragment were required."

"One thing is sure," offered Leroy. "Whoever wrote this letter to Homer and killed him may still have in his possession a copy of *Our Feathered Friends Down Under* with a triangular piece torn out of the last page."

"True," said Danforth. He stood up. "And now we know everything about Homer's murderer except his name, don't we?" He was half serious, half flippant.

Leroy said, "I think we ought to have a talk with the police when we get to New Zealand tomorrow."

"Okay," said Danforth. "But meanwhile, how about a short nap before cocktails?"

* * * *

A week later the *Valhalla* majestically steamed northward toward Suva in the Fiji Islands, her next port of call. It was dinnertime; the Viking Room was a cheerful hubbub of conversation, laughter, and dining sounds, The Danforths and Leroys had ordered dessert when a radiogram was delivered to their table by the radio officer. It was addressed to Martin Leroy.

Leroy tore it open. "It's from Detective Inspector Johnson in Wellington," he said, and proceeded to read its contents aloud:

"Happy to report murderer of *Valhalla* passenger Homer Rice arrested today. Positive evidence at hand that Milnor Van Allen, Associate Professor Zoology, local university, was in Tasmania at critical time for unexplained purpose; has recently settled sizable gambling debts with American currency; has corresponded Homer Rice for seven years and knew from recent letter Rice would be on *Valhalla* cruise calling Hobart Aug. 12. Also possesses copy *Our Feathered Friends Down Under* with mutilated last page into which triangular letter fits exactly. Van Allen's conviction for murder beyond doubt. Again, sincere thanks for your assistance.—Johnson, Det. Insp., Wellington."

They were silent for a few moments after he finished reading. Then Danforth said, "I don't suppose it makes any difference to Homer that they've caught his killer. But it makes me feel a lot better, I must say."

Leroy nodded. "I'll second that."

"So will I," chimed in Carol, "especially since I'm responsible for finding Homer's killer."

"You're responsible!" cried Danforth and Leroy together.

"Certainly," said Carol complacently. "I gave you the most important clue. I told you the murderer's name began with V."

Helen said, "I keep wondering and wondering about one thing. Could it be possible there still are some moa birds alive in those unexplored parts of New Zealand?"

Leroy and Danforth grinned at each other.

"Of course it's possible," said Danforth at length. "But if you ask me—"

Leroy finished for him: "'There aren't any moa any moa'."

The Philippine Key Mystery

Even in the most far-fetched fictional mystery written by the collaborative team of "Leroy King," a simple plate of fish soup had never led to the capture of a murderer. Yet in Zamboanga City, on the island of Mindanao in the Philippines, that's exactly what happened...

The cruise ship *Valhalla* anchored in Zamboanga Harbor early in the morning. Immediately most of her passengers debarked by tender for a long, hot, tiring day of sightseeing in the city and its environs. Now, with the cocktail hour upon them, the Danforths and the Leroys decided to have dinner ashore at the Bayot Hotel, attracted to this hostelry by its famous specialty, sinegang—a superb fish soup which King Danforth, a fancier of chowders, was eager to sample. They dined outdoors on a harborside terrace where the sea breeze intermittently afforded them some slight relief from the enervating heat that persisted even after sundown. And the sinegang, they unanimously agreed, was all that was claimed for it.

As they ate, a vinta, one of those outrigger canoes on which many Moros spend their entire lives, appeared out of the dusk of the harbor and nudged against the sea wall beside which their table was set. A man and woman, dark-skinned, both paddled the craft. A little girl of four or five years crouched amidships among the motley array of tourist goods which those sea gypsies had for sale.

With ingratiating grimaces and pleading words in incomprehensible Tagalog, the child held up one item after another to the Americans, urging them to buy: shirts of jusi and pina cloth, made from banana and pineapple fronds; hand-carved statuettes of a lemon-colored wood; bouquets of brilliant tropical blooms; glistening shells gathered from the sea bottom.

Helen Leroy was captivated at once by this small saleslady. "Oh, Mart," she said to her husband, "buy one of her shells for me, please. Isn't she a darling, Carol?"

Carol Danforth nodded. "And the only woman I've seen in Zamboanga who appears comfortably dressed for the climate," she said. The Moro child wore only a sketchy loincloth of a nondescript color—like the lower part of a bikini.

"Just what we need," said Martin Leroy. "A helmet shell from Zamboanga that must weigh five pounds if it weighs an ounce. With the dead animal still in it, too, I'll bet. I think I can smell it from here."

"A bunch of flowers then," urged Helen. "How can you possibly resist that innocent child? Are you completely heartless?"

Leroy stepped to the sea wall. "Flowers it is, then. How much for those flowers?" he asked the child, pointing.

A beatific smile transfigured the thin brown face. "Four pesos," she replied in perfect English. "Or one American dollar."

Danforth laughed. "Some innocent little salesgirl," he said. "I'll bet she speaks Spanish, too."

"Si. Si " the girl piped. "You want flowers? Please?"

"For a buck I'll take a chance," Leroy agreed. He fumbled in his pocket for the money.

"A dollar and a quarter if I dive," the child said quickly. "You got a quarter, Mister?"

The others joined Leroy at the sea wall. "What does she mean?" asked Carol.

"Dive," said the child. "In the water. Here." She handed up the flowers, accepted a dollar bill from Leroy, then passed it to her father. "Now throw quarter in water, sir. Sea very deep here. I dive for quarter and bring it up. You watch, yes?"

"Okay," said Leroy. He tossed a quarter out into the black water about five yards beyond the vinta.

Almost before it left his hand, the little girl arched over the canoe's outrigger in a clean pure dive. She stayed under for a few moments, then her head bobbed to the surface. She shook water from her hair. Holding one small hand aloft, she swam rapidly back to the canoe. By the smoky light of the lanterns that were spaced along the sea wall to illuminate the dining terrace and the water's edge, they could see the silver winking of Leroy's quarter in her uplifted palm.

"Wonderful!" Carol Danforth dapped her hands.

The child, all smiles, climbed back into the canoe, with water streaming from her brief bathing costume. Suddenly Danforth smothered an exclamation. "Do you see what I see?" he said to Leroy.

Leroy nodded. "Her—pants?" His eyes were intent.

"Yes." They both stared at the small diver's loincloth, lighted quite well now by the lantern light shining into the vinta.

"What are you two muttering about?" Helen Leroy asked, and then she broke off and stared too.

Carol gave an uncertain laugh. "The color?" she said. "Is that what's bothering you?"

Danforth said, "Unless I'm color blind, that's it."

"Masked by some vegetable dyes, maybe," Leroy offered, "but the real color comes through when it's wet."

Helen spoke indignantly. "You can't tell me that little five-year-old is a convicted criminal!"

"Maybe it's her father," Leroy said.

"Nonsense!" Carol joined Helen in protest. "It's a trick of the light, that's all."

Danforth said slowly, "Just the same, I'm going to call Señor Bollo."

* * * *

Señor Bollo was the Governor of San Ramon Penal Colony, situated a few miles outside Zamboanga. They had met him only a few hours before, while sipping tea in the grateful shade of an awning directly across the road from the forbidding stone entrance to the prison farm. Their Cruise Director had brought the prison governor to their table and introduced him.

"And these people," the Director had finished, "are the Danforths and the Leroys, Señor Bollo. You may have heard of the two gentlemen. They write crime fiction under the pen name of 'Leroy King.'"

Señor Bollo, short and coffee-colored, inclined politely from the waist. "I have indeed heard of Leroy King," he said. "As who has not? This is a great pleasure, sirs." His English was excellent. "Even here in Zamboanga your fame is known."

"Won't you sit down, Señor Bollo?" asked Helen Leroy, extending a slender hand in invitation. "You might as well, because our husbands will probably want to ask you a million questions about your prison." She nodded toward it. "We've just been given the grand tour, you know."

Bollo took the empty chair at their table. The Cruise Director excused himself and shot off on another errand. Carol Danforth poured Señor Bollo a cup of tea.

The prison governor waved a hand at the sapphire sea sparkling in the sunlight a hundred yards away, at the strip of white beach that edged it, at the gently swaying palm trees which sheltered the terrace on which they sat. "Have you ever seen a high security prison in a more beautiful setting?" he asked with pride in his voice.

"Never," said Helen, flashing him her devastating smile. "I'd almost be willing to be one of your prisoners, Señor, just for the view alone!"

With unmistakable warmth the prison official said, "And I would welcome you as one of my prisoners, Mrs. Leroy!" His glance paid silent homage to her blonde beauty.

King Danforth rubbed a palm over his crewcut and burrowed in his chair to get more comfortable. "Judging from our tour of your prison, Señor Bollo, you run a model institution."

Bollo bowed courteously. "Thank you."

"And judging from your handicraft shops and extensive gardens, you place a great deal of emphasis on rehabilitation, don't you?" Martin Leroy asked.

"We do," admitted the governor. "Second only to the emphasis we place on security, of course. One remembers, Mr. Leroy, that most of our prisoners here are murderers." Momentarily his words caused a slight chill to temper the heat of the afternoon. Carol shivered.

Helen said, "Goodness! Then I withdraw my offer to become a prisoner!"

Bollo bared large, square, very white teeth in a delighted grin. "I am desolate, Mrs. Leroy!"

Leroy put down his teacup with a careful impatience which showed how much he would have preferred cold beer to hot tea. "I'm curious about those prison pens inside the compound walls, Señor," he said. "The prisoners sleep there? And live there when not working?"

"Yes," said Bollo. "They are quite comfortable."

"But they're very insecure-looking for a high security prison," Danforth protested. "Walls of vertical bamboo bars four inches apart! That doesn't seem adequate somehow to confine desperate criminals. Why, even a persistent termite—"

Bollo held up a hand in amusement. "Wait. Those bamboo bars are very much stronger than they look, I assure you. They keep our convicts safely confined while allowing them to sleep and live in the open air. Our climate here, you understand, makes enclosed prison cells, such as yours in the States, intolerable. The heat would kill our prisoners. So we use those pens, walled with bars of bamboo—" he smiled—"and periodically we check for termites."

"Oh," said Danforth.

"Yes. The prisoners sleep on floor mats, communally. So

only one door is required for each pen, you see? And that one door is fitted with a huge metal lock to which only the particular guard assigned to that pen has the key. He lets the twenty prisoners in his pen out in the morning and he locks them in again at night. During working hours, of course, the prisoners are shackled together. It is a very fine system. Very safe."

"No home-baked cakes with little saw blades in them," Helen asked, "passed through the bars by devoted wives?"

Bollo smiled and shook his head. "No. And furthermore, before he is locked into his pen at night, each prisoner is carefully searched for anything that could possibly serve as a weapon or an escape tool. So you see, escape is impossible."

Leroy said, "Impossible? Do you mean that no prisoner has ever escaped from your San Ramon prison, Señor?"

Bollo flushed and looked unhappy. "Never," he said after a brief pause, torn between pride and truth, "except once."

"Ah," said Danforth, "then one criminal did make it?"

"Yes. In shame I confess it. A month ago, for the first time on record. A murderer named Antonio Taal. A man who had callously decapitated a fellow pearl diver in a fit of temper. Your pardon, ladies." Helen and Carol abruptly pushed back their teacups. Danforth and Leroy sat forward in their chairs, their faces mirroring intense professional interest.

Danforth said eagerly, "Tell us about it, Señor."

"There is very little to tell. This Antonio Taal worked in the wood-carver's shop which you no doubt visited today. He slept in pen Number Three. One night, after the search of his person which is nightly routine, he was locked into his pen with the other nineteen convicts in his group. The next morning when the guard for pen Number Three went to release the prisoners for breakfast, Taal was gone. Utterly. He had disappeared into thin air. Just like that. Bollo snapped his blunt fingers with a report that made Helen jump.

"Only Taal?" Leroy asked. "No other prisoner was missing from that pen?"

"None. And not a single bamboo bar was broken or damaged. And the pen door was still locked as securely as ever."

"A miracle," said Carol. "More tea, Señor Bollo?"

"Thank you."

Helen said, "I have two ideas about your murderer's escape, Señor Bollo. Associating with Leroy King all these years, you can understand that some of their deductive genius, in quotes, question mark, has rubbed off on Mrs. Danforth and me. Shall I explain Antonio Taal's escape for you?"

Bollo crinkled his eyes and showed his teeth. He was greatly taken with Helen. "Please do so," he begged.

"Well, first of all, I think that Antonio Taal was on a hunger strike over some fancied grievance. Was he?"

"No," said Bollo. "I am sorry. He always ate like a pig."

"Oh. I was going to say that a rigid diet could have made the prisoner so thin that he could have squeezed out of his pen between the bars. If, of course, he happened to have a rather small skull to begin with."

Bollo was convulsed with merriment. "Only four inches between bars," he said through his laughter. "What is your second idea, please?"

"My second idea," said Helen, "would be to interrogate the guard for pen Number Three pretty darn carefully."

Danforth and Leroy grinned at each other. "She has something there," Leroy said.

"We did, Mrs. Leroy," Bollo said, sobering. "At great length. And without result. He was able to prove conclusively that neither he nor his key to pen Number Three had been out of the guard's dormitory all night. Under severe interrogation every one of Taal's penmates denied seeing or hearing anything during the night that could have any bearing on Taal's escape."

"Then," said Leroy quickly, "it becomes simply a matter of a duplicate key, doesn't it?"

"No." Bollo was positive. "For the simple reason that a duplicate key could not conceivably have escaped detection whether it had been hidden on Taal's person or in his prison pen. The keys to our pens are no delicate, flat little space-savers, you understand. They are massive. Their stems are three inches long and curved like a half moon; their loops are an inch across; the pins and webs below the collar are made of iron a quarter of an inch thick. Not an easy key to conceal, you must see that. And I assure you that our daily searches of the convicts' quarters and persons—" he cast a sidelong look of faint embarrassment at the ladies—"are thorough in the extreme."

Señor Bollo paused reflectively before continuing. "Even if Taal somehow obtained a duplicate key and somehow succeeded in hiding it until the night of his escape, how, I have asked myself a thousand times, did he manage to get over the prison wall that surrounds the compound? You can see it from here. It is eleven feet high and has that projecting inner catwalk for guard patrol built along its top all the way around the compound. With a ladder or a rope that wall conceivably might be scaled from the inside. But not by a man who had neither. And not by a man who had a seriously injured foot."

"An injured foot?" Leroy pounced.

"Yes. A knife cut between the big toe and second toe of his right foot. Sometime before his escape he had accidentally dropped his woodcarving knife in the shop while working. The knife fell point down, penetrating his bare foot deeply. To complicate matters, the cut became infected, crippling Taal to the point where he needed a walking stick to get around at all—even the short distances between his pen, the workshop, and the dining barracks."

"Do guards patrol the wall all night?" Danforth asked.

"One guard. With a submachine gun. He patrols the catwalk continuously. At any sign of trouble he signals the guards on the main gate to turn on the floodlights, illuminating the whole compound as brightly as day. No such warning occurred the night of Taal's disappearance."

For a few moments no one spoke. A vagrant breath of air from the sea made the fronds of the palm trees rattle. With a conspiratorial twisting of the lips Leroy looked at Danforth and grinned.

Danforth said, "Señor Bollo, your escaped prisoner—this is the kind of problem that my partner and I concern ourselves with constantly in plotting our mystery stories. We find the discussion and analysis of such puzzles stimulating. They help us to make our living. Will you therefore forgive what may seem like an impertinence to you, and let the two of us speculate on your puzzle? I think we can explain how Antonio Taal escaped."

It was Bollo's turn to sit forward in his chair. "You are joking, surely. You seriously think you can solve a mystery in ten minutes that my staff and I have been working on for four weeks without success?" His square teeth showed a grin that now had a hint of derision.

"Yes," Leroy murmured, his sunburned face assuming the bland expression that his wife called his Q.E.D. look. "Yes, I think we can."

"Please don't take offense, Señor Bollo," Helen said hastily, putting a hand on his sleeve. "You are dealing here, don't forget, with a two-headed professional mystery computer into which, or into whom, you merely feed the known facts of your puzzle and out of which, or out of whom, the solution is inevitably belched forth!"

Leroy patted her knee under the table. "Isn't that a rather indelicate description of your husband and his partner?"

Carol said, "Yes, Señor Bollo, we apologize for them." She looked around for a waiter. "Don't they serve anything but tea in this place, for heaven's sake?" Her voice was plaintive.

Danforth lit a cigarette and blew smoke into the overheated air. "I can see you're skeptical, Señor Bollo. And I don't blame you. Will you let us try, however? And answer just one more question first?"

"It will be my pleasure." Bollo had the air of a man trying to go along with a gag thought up by idiot children.

"This walking stick used by Taal to hobble about on," said Danforth. "Was he allowed to take it into his pen with him at night?"

"He was. He could not walk without it. And it is sometimes necessary, you understand, for a prisoner to get up at night..." Bollo let his words trail off, again glancing self-consciously at the ladies.

"A fact of nature," Leroy said sententiously, "and not to be denied, even in a prison pen. Exactly what kind of walking stick did Taal use?"

Bollo pointed at the souvenir walking stick that Helen Leroy had purchased an hour before from a shackled woodcarver in the prison shop. "One of those," Bollo said. "The kind Taal himself carved for sale to tourists."

Danforth, in high spirits, struck the table a light blow. "I thought so," he said. "You begin, Mart."

Leroy nodded. "Señor Bollo. Taal was a woodcarver in your prison shop. So he must have been skilled with a knife."

"Skilled enough to cut off a pal's head over a pearl," Carol offered.

"Quiet," Leroy admonished her. "I was saying. Antonio Taal undoubtedly made the duplicate key to pen Number Three himself. Carved it out of wood, at odd moments when he was unobserved in the shop."

Bollo started to protest. Danforth interrupted him. "Wait, now, give us a chance. Taal saw the guard's key to pen Number Three hundreds of times, eh? A keen observer could have registered its size, shape, and general configuration quite accurately after a few years of looking at it every day, couldn't he? And kept the details in his memory? Besides, Taal also had the lock itself, into which the key fitted, before his eyes every day. So he decided to try his hand at carving a key that would lead him to freedom. Isn't that a reasonable assumption."

"Impossible."

"Not at all." Leroy took up the argument. "You are going to say, where could Taal keep his wooden key while he was laboriously carving it over a period of many weeks so that no guard or other prisoner would suspect its existence?"

"Where?" said Bollo. "Exactly."

"In the handle of one of the walking sticks he was carving in the shop," Danforth supplied the answer promptly. He reached out and took Helen's walking stick which was hanging by its handle over the back of her chair.

It was a handsome cane. A thick curved hand-grip, shaped like the grip of a revolver, topped a stout stick of beautifully carved mahogany. The stick tapered in a graceful series of octagonal, round, and spiral sections to a slender ferrule. Its entire length was embellished with bands, studs, and floral designs of mother-of-pearl, delicately inlaid in the wood. The butt end of the stick's grip was faced with a large oval lozenge of mother-of-pearl, two inches in length and one inch in width.

"He hollowed out the handle of one of these sticks," Danforth went on. "Made a cavity big enough to hold the duplicate key. Then he covered the cavity with a big wafer of mother-of-pearl like this one, easily removable, easily replaced. And he merely refrained from finishing the carving and decoration of that particular stick so it would not be sold to a tourist before he was ready to use the key inside its handle."

"But," said Señor Bollo, still humoring these odd Americans, "he could not have known that his wooden key would actually turn the pen lock. Not possibly. The chances of carving from memory a key that would fit the lock are a million to one!"

"True," Leroy admitted. "So Taal made sure that the key he was carving would fit."

"How?"

"By deliberately cutting his foot with his carving knife," Leroy said. "How else?"

"Oh, come now," Bollo said indulgently. "It was an accident. There was nothing deliberate about it. The other woodcarvers in the shop testified to that."

"Naturally," Danforth said. "Taal meant it to look like an accident. But we would be naive to believe it, wouldn't we? A man so skilled in handling a knife as Taal? No. He cut his foot on purpose. And infected it deliberately, too, I'll bet, so that your prison doctor would recommend that he be allowed to use a cane. In any event, he was permitted to use the cane, wasn't he?"

"He was."

"So what have we?" Danforth spoke with relish. "A convicted murderer, a crippled murderer, with a wooden key to his pen door concealed in his cane's handle. And a natural need, like all of us, to get up at night occasionally. Surreptitiously on these occasions he tries his key, removed from the cane handle, in the lock of the pen door. And guided by these clandestine nocturnal tests, he adds refinements, the finishing touches, to the web of his carved key next day in the shop. Finally one night the key works when he tries it in the pen lock. He thereupon seizes the first opportunity, when all his penmates are sound asleep, to unlock the door of the pen, hobble out cane in hand, relock the door from the outside, and make himself scarce. It could be, couldn't it, Señor Bollo?"

Bollo shook his head. "What of the compound wall?" He pointed dramatically across the road. "What of the patrolling guard on top of the wall? And how could a crippled man, whose foot was agony to touch to the ground, possibly run far enough to escape?—even if he did miraculously manage to get over the wall."

"That's not too difficult to explain," Leroy said placidly. He and Danforth were enjoying themselves. "One guard patrolling the catwalk on top of the wall means there would be intervals of several minutes between his successive visits to any specific point on the perimeter. Especially if he walks clear around the compound on each pass, as you say he does. Antonio Taal, it seems to me, would merely time the guard's patrol and go over the wall while the guard was on the other side of the compound. Simple."

"How?" asked Bollo, beginning to perspire. "How did he scale the wall?"

"How tall was Taal?" Danforth asked.

"Perhaps five and a half feet."

"Figure it out then," Danforth said. "If he's five and a half feet tall, he probably has a reach of about seven feet, give or take a couple of inches, when he stands on tiptoe and reaches upward. Add to this the three-foot length of the walking stick in his hand. And the few desperate inches he could force himself to jump off his uninjured foot. Holding his cane by its ferrule end, and using the handle of the stick as a hook to catch over the inner rail of the catwalk on the wall's top, an agile man could climb up his cane, hand over hand, and reach the top of an eleven foot wall quite easily. And descend the same way on the other side." Danforth winked at Leroy. "Was Taal an agile man, Señor Bollo?"

Bollo coughed. "Yes," he said slowly. "He was as muscular as a monkey."

"Which, incidentally, have no tails in Zamboanga, I understand," Carol murmured.

Bollo exclaimed, almost to himself, "By our Lady of Pillar! Yes. Yes. It is barely possible." He half stood, then sat again, looking crestfallen. "But no," he said, his coffee-colored face solemn, "not with a foot like Taal's. He could not have traveled a quarter of a mile from here by morning—even if he had crawled on his belly. Yet the greatest manhunt Zamboanga ever saw combed every rock, beach, blade of grass, and patch of jungle within a ten-mile radius of this prison within six hours after Taal was discovered missing, and no trace of him was found. Nor was any cart, car, boat, or outrigger in which he might have escaped reported missing."

He broke off abruptly as a file of men in shapeless garments of an odd, orange-russet color trudged slowly down the road toward the prison gate, trying to walk in step through their own dust. The chains connecting them leg to leg made a metallic clinking, plainly audible to the tea drinkers under the awning opposite the gate. A guard carrying a shotgun walked beside the file of prisoners.

"A road gang coming in for dinner," Bollo said, gesturing. Then, "And that is another thing. Those prison clothes—"

Helen interrupted him. "They're a darling color, Señor Bollo. Such a chic orangy-red! I wish I could buy some of that cloth to take home with me. It would make awfully cute slacks, Carol."

Bollo showed his big white teeth. "I'm afraid that is out of the question, Mrs. Leroy. The cloth is not available to the public. Only my prisoners wear it. Its color is unique, as you say. That special orange dye is used only for prison material. Very high visibility color, do you see? Anyone wearing clothes of that color is instantly recognized as a convicted criminal. That is what I meant, gentleman—another puzzling factor about Taal's escape. Dressed in prison clothes of that color, he would have stood out like a shark among pilot fish. Yet no one in Zamboanga saw him."

He shrugged and smiled at Helen. "I think you are right, after all, Mrs. Leroy. More right than your husband. Antonio Taal starved himself to nothing and was spirited out of my prison camp to heaven, a disembodied ghost."

Leroy laughed. "There's a simpler explanation than that. I think you may have inadvertently overlooked one important fact in connection with your murderer."

"What fact is that?"

"He was a pearl diver," Leroy said. "Therefore an excellent swimmer. A man used to the water, at home in the sea. I think he swam away from your prison by night, when his orange clothing could not be seen, and laid up for rest at daylight in some lonely cove along the shore between here and Zamboanga City." Leroy thumbed at the murmuring surf a few yards away. "We saw plenty of likely spots as we drove out here today along the coast road. And a very good swimmer could easily swim ten miles before daybreak in a calm sea if he escaped from the pen in the middle of the night."

Explosively Señor Bollo called once again on Pillar, patron saint of Zamboanga. The expression on his face was a comic mixture of sudden enlightenment and chagrin, mixed with anger, astonishment, and at last, healthy amusement. When Danforth added innocently, "And as for Taal's infected foot, its long immersion in salt water might have proved most beneficial," the amusement won out over his other emotions, and Bollo laughed heartily.

"A remarkable reconstruction," he said, "thoroughly worthy of Leroy King. If it happened that way, of course."

Danforth grinned. "It may be a little far-fetched," he conceded, "but it is not at all incredible."

"In any event," Bollo said, "Taal escaped and is still at large. He is a brutal, short-tempered murderer who will almost certainly kill again. If I could get him back in San Ramon prison before he does so, I would be a very happy man."

* * * *

"So here's to a very happy man," said Danforth, taking a sip of his nightcap. It was shortly after midnight.

They sat in the Horseshoe Bar of the *Valhalla*, now breathing the long swells of the Celebes Sea, Borneo-bound. "To Señor Bollo, who has his wandering murderer safely behind bamboo bars once more."

"Thanks to our sharp eyes and sharper minds," said Leroy self-satisfiedly.

Helen bristled. "Thanks to a four-year-old child, you mean!"

"What?" Danforth was bland. "Just because the kid happened to be diving and found Taal's orange convict suit on the sea bottom, weighted down with rocks under some widow's house in the Mohammedan settlement? And told Bollo where it was so he could raid the place earlier tonight?"

"Isn't that enough?" Helen said. "They caught the escaped murderer there, didn't they? Terrorizing the widow into feeding and hiding him!"

"True. But what about the child's mother, if it comes to a question of who's responsible for catching Taal? She's the one who made bathing trunks for her youngster out of the orange material the kid found." Danforth winked at his partner. "And if we hadn't noticed the color of the child's bikini—"

"Which brings us back to those sharp eyes I mentioned," said Leroy. "Ours."

"Then your sharp eyes are also responsible, I take it," said Carol with some spirit, "for the poor constable's arm that Antonio Taal broke with that while resisting arrest." She pointed to a walking stick Leroy held between his knees—a parting gift from Señor Bollo. Behind a large disk of mother-of-pearl in the hollow handle of the cane the prison governor had found the duplicate key—a massive key crudely carved out of hardwood.

"It seems to me," murmured Leroy soothingly, "that perhaps the best case of all could be made for the fish soup."

"I know it is undignified to bicker with one's wives," remarked Danforth with the air of a man much put upon, "but simple justice requires me to point out, all the same, that Leroy King's reconstruction of the escape was flawless."

Helen laughed. "Yes, but it was a very simple puzzle," she said. "Why, even stupid little me had several perfectly good explanations."

"Yeah," her husband jeered affectionately. "Between you and Bollo you had Taal starving himself to death and rising up to heaven as a disembodied spirit! Is that what you call a perfectly good explanation ?"

Danforth chuckled. "You know something? I would have favored that theory too, except for one thing."

"What?"

"I just couldn't seem to picture a disembodied spirit wearing orange pants!"

The Borneo Snapshot Mystery

King Danforth couldn't sleep.

The Norwegian cruise ship *Valhalla*, in spite of her widely advertised stabilizers, was rolling heavily as she forged through the South China Sea toward Hong Kong. It was 5:30 in the morning; the *Valhalla* was forty hours out of Jesselton, her most recent port of call; and King lay in his bunk, wide-awake. His wife, Carol, was still asleep.

Without awakening her he slid out of bed, donned slacks, jersey, and sandals, quietly opened their cabin door, and emerged on the sun deck. A glance showed him that he had the ship to himself. Not even a Norwegian deckhand was in evidence. The rising sun revealed the eastern horizon as a faintly rosy undulating line between the sky and the heaving sea.

He walked aft, toward the sunrise, feeling proud of the sea legs he had acquired in half a hundred days at sea. He needed them this morning—to counter the unpredictable movements of the deck under his feet. Ten-foot seas, he judged, the aftermath of a week-old typhoon in whose wake they sailed.

Reaching the rail at the aft end of the sun deck, he decided to descend to the main deck for his stroll and moved to the head of the railed staircase that led down to it.

It was just as he started down the stairs that he saw the body.

A man lay asprawl on the deck at the foot of the steps, supine, limbs slack and disordered, a macabre study in black and white: black hair, black dinner jacket, and black shoes; white face and ruffled white shirt front. King's instant conjecture was that some elderly or possibly drunken passenger, trying to negotiate the staircase in the heavy seas, had fallen headlong down the stairs.

He ran down the steps and bent over the man, feeling for a pulse and trying to recognize the upturned face. It was familiar but not one to which he could attach a name. Nor could he find a pulse in the thin wrist. When he looked at the man's face again, he understood why. A horizontal depression, deep enough to lay a finger in, ran across the man's forehead just below the hairline, with an area of bruised and dusty skin around it.

King rose slowly to his feet. No use listening for a heartbeat. That massive skull fracture left no doubt the man was dead.

* * * *

When King and his wife joined Martin and Helen Leroy in the dining room for breakfast, King told them all about it. The Leroys were jolted by the news. The death of any member of a ship's company is always unsettling—a far more immediate reminder of man's mortality than a random death ashore.

"His name was Calvin Speaker, apparently," Danforth finished "We've seen him around on the cruise—at informative talks and on shore excursions and so on. You know him, Mart?"

Leroy shook his head. "Calvin Speaker? Nope. Can't place him."

"Bushy guardsman-type mustache, long sideburns, patent-leather hair," Danforth said.

Helen spoke up. "I think I know who he was. Quite handsome in a dark saturnine way. He used to sit beside the dance floor evenings, drinking Brandy Alexanders and staring at me a lot."

Her husband chuckled. "Everybody does," he said. He was proud of her good looks.

"He was traveling alone," Danforth said, "according to

the passenger list. Mr. Calvin Speaker from Sacramento."

Carol murmured, "Poor man! It's sad to die alone and so far away from home."

Martin Leroy gave his partner a curious look. "Listen, King, how come this news hasn't hit the ship's rumor mill yet?"

"The doctor asked me to keep it quiet until next of kin is notified and official cause of death determined—you know the routine. Then the Captain will announce it."

"Cause of death!" Helen caught him up. "I thought you said he fell down the steps and cracked his head."

"Yeah," Martin Leroy said. "Didn't he?"

"The doctor thinks so."

"Don't you?" Leroy stared at his friend. "What are you hinting at?"

Helen curled her beautiful lips. "Now don't tell me there's something mysterious about this! Just because you two write mystery stories, you surely aren't looking for a plot in a poor lonely man falling down the stairs!"

King rubbed a big hand over his hair and reached for another piece of toast. "There were a couple of odd things about Calvin Speaker's death."

"Odd?" Leroy asked.

"The guy still had his dinner jacket on, for one thing."

"At five-thirty this morning?"

"Right." On the *Valhalla* it was *de rigueur* to dress for dinner every night at sea except Sundays.

"What else?" asked Leroy.

"He had dust on his forehead."

Helen said, "You're trying to make something out of that?"

Danforth put marmalade on his toast and shrugged.

Leroy said, "Because he still had his dinner jacket on, King, you think he fell down the stairs last night?"

Danforth nodded.

"So what's odd about that?" Helen wanted to know.

"If he fell down the steps last night, the night watchman or a deckhand should have found him long before I did this morning. They scrub down the decks every night, you know. And the night watchman makes four complete rounds of the ship, inside and out, every night."

Leroy nodded. "And what's odd about Speaker having dust on his forehead?"

"Yes," his wife chimed in, "isn't it perfectly natural for a man who falls down a whole flight of steps to get some dust on his head?"

Danforth answered almost reluctantly. "Not on this ship, it isn't. They keep it cleaner than a baby's crib. I rubbed my finger over those stair treads this morning and got no dust at all. Not a speck."

Leroy, munching his third buckwheat cake, said, "Excellent procedural technique, my boy. Under the circumstances I agree that dust was extremely odd. What did Dr. Hagen say?"

"He didn't say what he was obviously thinking—that I was out of my skull to ask about a spot of dust on a dead man's forehead."

Helen gave King a dazzling smile. "My respect for the doctor rises, darling. He's a fine diagnostician to recognize you so quickly as a mental case."

"Thanks." Danforth grinned. "I love it when you're sweet to me like that. Is Helen sweet to you too, Mart?"

"Never," Leroy confessed. "But then, she's my wife."

Carol snapped, "Stop that horrible joking when poor Mr. Speaker is hardly cold yet!"

"You bring up an important point," Leroy said. "How about that, King? Any rigor mortis when you found him?"

"Some. Dr. Hagen thought it was ghoulish of me to ask about that too."

"I like the doctor better all the time," Helen said.

King continued, "So I compromised. I suppressed my curiosity about rigor mortis and settled for a promise from the doc that he'd take a look at that funny gray dust on Speaker's forehead."

"You mean under a microscope?"

"Exactly. And report his findings—" Danforth looked toward the dining-room entrance. "There's Dr. Hagen now. Excuse me." He got up and went over to the doorway. The others watched him greet the tall ship's doctor. Dr. Hagen said something to Danforth, then shook his head and turned away. King came back to the table and sat down. "He had to get back to the sick bay."

Leroy said, "How about the dust on Speaker's forehead?"

"You'll never guess what it was."

"I will," Carol said. "I figured it out long ago. Dandruff."

"Quiet, woman," Leroy commanded, "while two mature minds wrestle with this odd discrepancy in an otherwise run-of-the-mill accident. Well, King?"

"The dust on Speaker's forehead seemed to consist of—get this—tiny colored glass spheres."

Silence greeted this announcement. Then Helen said, "There goes my newfound respect for the doctor. He's a mental case himself."

"Did he say anything else, King?" Leroy asked.

"Just not to bother him any more. In a nice way, of course," Martin Leroy said with the enthusiasm of the true puzzle-solver, "What, may I ask, are a bunch of microscopic glass spheres doing on board a ship at sea, let alone on a dead man's forehead?"

"How about that glassy powder on a nail file?" Carol offered. "You know, like sandpaper?"

"Or some of that shiny stuff in a city sidewalk? Mica, is it?" Helen said.

Danforth shook his head. "Sorry, ladies. They aren't spheres. And besides, the doctor said colored glass spheres. Red, blue, and green."

"Oh, colored!" Helen was undismayed. "How about some of the stuff on one of those sparkly masks they wear in Rio for the Carnival?"

Leroy suddenly put down his fork with a clatter. His dark eyes glowed. "Please," he begged, "will you dispense with these childish guessing games for a moment? And let the genius in your midst be heard?"

"Mart, you know what the dust is?"

"I thought you'd never ask. Of course I know what it is. Anyone with a reasonably keen interest in amateur photography would know. At least," he amended with a broad deprecatory smile, "anyone who has total recall like me."

"Total recall!" Helen scoffed. "Why, you can't even remember your social-security number!"

Danforth said, "Please ignore your unappreciative wife, Mart. What's the dust?"

Leroy narrowed his eyes dramatically. "The dust is the material they coat on home movie screens."

"Hey!" Danforth exclaimed. "Now you mention it, I think that's it. To make the surface reflective, right?"

"We're very impressed," Carol said, "but so what?"

Her husband answered, "It just might mean that Calvin Speaker didn't fall down those steps at all."

"Here we go again!" Helen moaned. "You mean he may have been murdered, I suppose?"

"Maybe. Or at least killed somewhere else than on that staircase."

"Like where?"

"Like somebody's cabin where there's a home movie screen."

"I can see what's coming next," Carol announced.

"Killed last night in somebody's cabin where there's a home movie screen, kept in the cabin all night, then brought out on deck and pushed down those steps to make it look like an accident."

"You're beginning to learn, my dear," said Leroy. "No doubt by association with your brilliant husband, my partner. But that would account for the dinner jacket at daybreak and the dust on the forehead."

Helen laughed. "I can think of another way to account, for the dinner jacket. And not necessarily involving a movie screen, either."

"You mean he spent the night in some blonde's cabin?" her husband asked. "Some sordid shipboard intrigue. Forget it. We've got a great clue here that could mean murder. So let's not get side-tracked by romance."

"Spoken like a true mystery fan," agreed Danforth. "So who on board would have a home movie screen in his cabin?"

"Almost anybody," Helen said.

"No, it's unlikely that any of the passengers would bring a movie screen on a cruise. Cameras, yes. Screen, no."

"How about the crew?" Carol suggested.

Her husband shook his head "Not likely."

"Listen." Leroy took over. "How about narrowing it down, for the nonce, to the likeliest possibility?"

"The ship's photographer," Danforth said. "Okay."

"Gregory?" Helen asked. "That nice youngster?"

"That nice youngster with a movie screen in his cabin which I have personally seen."

"But he wouldn't kill anyone!"

"I don't think he would, either," Leroy murmured. "All the same I'd like to examine Gregory's movie screen."

* * * *

After breakfast they took a leisurely turn around the promenade deck. As they passed the bulletin board on which the ship's photographer posted the candid shots he took during shore excursions, Danforth said, "Wait a minute, Mart. Maybe there's a picture of Calvin Speaker here." They stopped and scanned the rows of photographs pinned to the board.

The latest batch covered the *Valhalla*'s visit to Jesselton, North Borneo. The Leroys and Danforths had already seen the display—had, indeed, ordered two prints from the ship's photographer as keepsakes of the cruise: a shot of the four of them grouped around a heavy-horned water buffalo.

The whole Jesselton shore trip was represented. Tanjong Aru beach, from which had been visible the towering jungled mountain on which the fast-disappearing orangutan was making its last stand against extinction; the unicorn and lion dances performed by Malay and Chinese children; the rubber plantations, rice fields, native villages; the water-buffalo races at Penampang; the exhibition of blowgun marksmanship by a Murut native. In almost every scene one or more cruise passengers appeared, but in none of them could they spot the face of Mr. Calvin Speaker.

Leroy indicated an empty space in one of the rows of photographs. "There's no picture number 432," he said with a quick glance at Danforth, "although apparently there was one, judging from the thumbtack hole in the board."

Flanking the empty space were two pictures—numbers 431 and 433—of cruise passengers standing beside the naked Murut tribesman who had demonstrated the accuracy of his blowgun by placing breath-expelled darts neatly in a small pig-shaped target forty yards away. The savage, flamboyant in feathered plumes and nothing else, was selling blowguns to the fascinated tourists from a small bundle of guns at his feet.

"Do you suppose," asked Danforth carefully, "that the missing photo number 432 could be a picture of Calvin Speaker? And that it has been, for some unknown reason, removed from this display?"

"There's one way to find out," Leroy replied. "And we wanted to look at Gregory's movie screen anyway."

King cleared his throat. "May we meet you two charmers in our deck chairs shortly?" he said to the wives. "We are about to undertake negotiations of the utmost delicacy and can't permit ourselves to be distracted by two beautiful women."

With the haughty air of dowagers denied an invitation to the fete of the season, Carol and Helen went off to their deck chairs while Leroy and Danforth thoughtfully made their way to the ship's photographer's cabin-cum-darkroom on the main deck.

Danforth knocked. After a moment Gregory opened the door halfway and peered out into the corridor. "Yes?" he inquired. Then he recognized them, and his somewhat distraught expression sharpened into a welcoming smile. "What can I do for you?"

"May we come in for a minute, Greg?" Leroy asked. "Got a little problem."

"Sure." Gregory stepped aside and they went in past him. He waved at his bunk. "Sit down. What's your problem? Do you need a photographic consultant on your next plot?" Like almost everyone on the *Valhalla*, Gregory knew that his two visitors were the famous literary collaboration known as "Leroy King," whose books have sold more than 125,000,000 copies throughout the world. "If so, I'm your man."

Danforth and Leroy ranged themselves side by side on the edge of his bunk. Gregory remained standing, his back to the door. "We've got two problems, actually," Danforth said.

Gregory, faintly red of eye and uneasy of manner," said, "Let's have 'em. I'll present my bill for expert advice later." He was obviously keeping it light.

Leroy said, "First problem: I want to show some color slides in my cabin. May I borrow your movie screen?"

Gregory shook his head regretfully. "I'm sorry, but it's broken, Mr. Leroy. Fell over during the rough seas last night and got a tear in it."

"Oh? A bad one?"

"Pretty bad. Too big a tear to be of much use. I'm afraid. Look, I'll show you." Gregory stooped and pulled a rolled-up screen from under the bunk. "I had it set up in here last night to run through a few of my own slides," he explained, "and a big wave tipped it over." He pulled the screen out of its cylindrical metal housing. "See?"

There was a long rough-edged slit near the center of the unrolled screen.

Leroy said, "Some of the reflective coating has even been knocked off." He pointed to the tear in the screen. "See that smooth spot?" He stood up as though to leave. "Well, thanks anyway, Greg."

"Wait a minute, Mart," said Danforth. "I want to ask about that picture."

Leroy sat down again. Gregory moved his feet restlessly on the carpet. "What picture?" Gregory inquired.

Danforth said, "I want to order a print of picture number 432, Greg. From the prom deck bulletin board."

With a brusque movement Gregory pushed himself away from the door against which he was leaning. His ruddy face lost some of its color. With a visible effort he said, "What number was that, Mr. Danforth?"

"432."

"432? What do you want with that one? My whole 430 series just shows the Borneo blowgun man with various passengers, that's all. You weren't in any of them."

Danforth said slowly, "I want a picture of Calvin Speaker, Greg. He was a very nice chap, we all thought." Very slightly he emphasized the past tense.

Gregory slumped against the door bonelessly and closed his eyes for a moment. Leroy and Danforth watched him in silence. At length the photographer said, "I should have had better sense. When I saw you two at the door I had a feeling you knew. But damn it, I didn't kill him!"

"Didn't you?" Leroy asked softly.

"No! But who'll believe me?"

"Maybe we will. Why'd you fake the accident if you didn't kill him—the falling-down-the-stairs bit?"

Gregory licked his lips. "Why? Isn't it obvious? What

do you think my job on this ship would be worth if I naively reported to the Captain that one of his passengers was lying dead of a fractured skull on the floor of my cabin? I'd be blacklisted forever as a ship's photographer, even if they didn't charge me with murder, for God's sake! Don't you realize that on a cruise the passenger is always right, the staff member never?" He rubbed a hand over his eyes, a gesture that emphasized his youth and vulnerability. "How'd you find out about the screen and picture number 432?"

Danforth told him. At the end Gregory said. "It would be my luck that you found the body. You, of all people. A detective-story writer, for God's sake!"

Danforth said grimly, "If you didn't kill Speaker, who did?"

"He killed himself, you might say." Gregory told the story in a monotone. At midnight the previous night, needing fresh film to photograph a birthday party in the bar, he had returned to his cabin and met Speaker just leaving it with one of Gregory's negatives in his hand. Quite naturally Gregory asked him what the hell he was doing in his cabin, meanwhile snatching the negative from him, pushing him back into the cabin, and closing the door.

Speaker had tried to apologize. Then, getting no encouragement from Gregory, he had surprisingly tried to buy the negative, offering Gregory one hundred dollars for it. This sum was so large that suspicion was immediately added to Gregory's anger, and he refused to sell. Whereupon Speaker, in a sudden fury, lunged across the narrow stateroom, intent, Gregory thought, on taking the negative from Gregory by force. His movement happened to coincide with a violent lurch of the ship in the heavy seas that were running, with the result that he was catapulted across the room, his head striking first against the movie screen erected at the foot of Gregory's bunk, and then, with sickening force, against the edge of the bunk.

"That's the God's truth," Gregory finished. "So help me. Do you believe me?"

Danforth answered obliquely. "Why'd you wait until dawn to dump him at the foot of the steps? His dinner jacket was what made me suspicious in the first place."

"Oh, lord!" Gregory said, stricken. "I never thought of the dinner jacket! The night steward was polishing passengers' shoes across from my door nearly all night long. I couldn't carry Speaker's body out of here until the steward went away."

"Where's the negative that Speaker was so anxious to get hold of?" Leroy asked. "Picture number 432, I suppose?"

"Yeah. Here it is." The photographer reached into a file beside the door. "Along with a print I made of it while I was waiting for the steward to leave last night. I thought it might explain Speaker's interest in it, but it's not much help. Just shows Speaker with the Borneo blowgun man."

Danforth stood up. "Let us have it for a while, will you?"

"Sure, take it." Gregory handed the print to Leroy. "You going to report me to the Captain? I suppose you have to."

"Not right away," Leroy answered after a glance at Danforth. "What do you say, King? Speaker's dead. And Greg can't go anywhere till we get to our next port, anyway. Personally I'm inclined to believe him about Speaker's death."

With Gregory's thanks echoing in their ears they went to their deck chairs on the lee side of the boat deck. Here, while Danforth told the girls about their talk with Gregory, Leroy studied Gregory's candid picture of Calvin Speaker and the naked blowgun marksman.

When Danforth finished his account he turned to his partner. "Does the photo give us anything?"

Leroy handed the print to Carol. "Just another tourist picture. Calvin Speaker buying one of those blowguns from the Murut."

Carol looked at the picture, passed it on to Helen. After a moment Helen said, "Speaker isn't looking at the Murut or his blowgun, really. He's looking over his shoulder, as if to see whether or not anyone's watching him."

"And smoothing back his hair with one hand," Danforth added.

"He looks sort of uneasy to me," Carol remarked.

"Why, for Pete's sake, would he be uneasy?" Danforth asked. "Buying a blowgun from a native isn't that shameful."

"The native is naked," pointed out Carol primly.

"Let me have a look," Danforth said. He took the print from Helen. After examining it he said, "Speaker not only looks uneasy, he looks different somehow."

"Different?" asked Leroy.

"Yeah. Different from the way he looked this morning when I found him at the foot of the steps."

"He was dead this morning," Carol reminded him. "And he was alive in that picture. There's a pretty big difference, if you ask me."

"I don't mean that. I mean Speaker's appearance is different in this picture."

"Let me have another look," Helen said. "I'm the only one of us who seems to have noticed poor Mr. Speaker before today."

Danforth handed her the photograph. She looked at it in silence. Then she turned to Danforth. "His forehead is too high," she said.

Danforth snatched the picture. "That's it—that's what's different. A higher forehead. His face seems too thin and long between those sideburns."

"Impossible," said Leroy. "A man's forehead doesn't expand or contract in a matter of forty-eight hours, King! Perhaps having his hand on his head in the picture changes the visual impression of his face."

Carol spoke up in a challenging tone. "I just thought of something," she said, "and I don't want either of you geniuses to take credit for it. Okay?"

"Okay." Danforth grinned at her. "The credit is entirely yours for whatever it is you've thought of. What is it?"

Carol said, "There is a way a man's forehead can grow higher—"

"I know how!" said Helen suddenly.

Carol went on as though she had not been interrupted. "I'll try not to be too technical about this, but when one is dealing with rudimentary intelligences—"

"Come on, come on," Leroy urged her. "What you're trying to say is that Speaker wore a hairpiece, aren't you? And in this picture the hairpiece has slipped back on his head a bit?"

"What I'm trying to say," Carol exclaimed with an indignant look at Leroy, "is that I'm going to join Women's Lib! Tomorrow!"

Danforth stared at the picture in his hand. "By George, that's it, Mart! Speaker's not smoothing back his hair—he's trying to hold it on! Or trying to resettle his hairpiece farther forward on his forehead!"

Leroy nodded. "It must have come loose from its moorings during the Borneo shore excursion."

"Poor Mr. Speaker was bald!" Helen said. "No wonder he's embarrassed in the picture. If your hairpiece suddenly came unstuck—"

Thoughtfully Leroy said, "Embarrassed? I'm not sure that's the right word."

"Why not?" demanded Carol. "Here's a man who wears a wig to conceal his baldness from his fellow passengers. And suddenly his wig comes loose. Wouldn't you be embarrassed?"

Danforth, still studying the snapshot," said, "I'd say Mr. Speaker looks more scared than embarrassed."

"Scared?" Helen said. "Why would he be scared? Or who would he be scared of?"

"There you have me," said Danforth. "But it's certainly not the blowgun salesman, naked or not."

"In view of the circumstances surrounding his demise," suggested Leroy, "I'd say he was scared of having his picture taken with his wig at half mast."

"Why?" asked Carol.

"Because he didn't want to be seen that way. To avoid it he was willing to try theft, bribery, assault, and possibly even murder on Gregory. Just to keep this picture out of circulation."

"Why?" asked Carol. "This is the last time I'll ask you."

"For fear somebody who saw this picture might recognize him. That seems to be obvious." Danforth gazed over the rail at the long foam-capped swells that paraded by the ship. "Recognize his true identity, that is."

"Whoa!" Helen said. "Are you saying that Calvin Speaker wasn't Calvin Speaker? That he was somebody else?"

"Could be," said Leroy judiciously. "Very probable, in fact. Give me another look at that picture, King." Then, after a moment's study, "The sideburns and mustache could be fake, too."

"Or recently grown," added Danforth, "to go with the wig."

Leroy brooded over the photograph in his hand. "At this point I could bear to take a look at Calvin Speaker's remains. Couldn't you?"

"We'd better go to the Captain, then," said Danforth, "because Dr. Hagen has had me and my curiosity up to here by now. He'll defend his domain from us with drawn sword, I'm afraid, unless the Captain intercedes."

* * * *

At pre-luncheon cocktails Leroy and Danforth reported to their wives.

"Captain Thorsen went with us," Danforth said, "so the doctor grudgingly let us look at Speaker before they put him in the—er—ship's freezer."

"Ghouls!" said Helen, shivering.

"The sideburns are genuine, but the mustache was fake, it turned out," said Leroy.

"So Calvin Speaker wasn't Calvin Speaker?"

"Right," said Leroy. He smiled at his wife.

She put her head on one side and regarded him narrowly. "You want me to ask who Calvin Speaker really was, don't you?"

"Please," said her husband, till smiling.

"All right, who was he?" Helen obliged him. "Anybody we know?"

"Nobody we know," said Danforth. "But old Mr. Total Recall, he knew him all right—once the doctor removed the wig and mustache."

Leroy nodded complacently. "It was child's play for me to identify this bald character known to us as Calvin Speaker."

Carol and Helen knew they were being baited. They also knew that Leroy did have an excellent memory. So his wife couldn't resist repeating her question: "Who was Calvin Speaker, Mart?"

"Clark Anselm," said Leroy.

Helen looked blank. So did Carol. "Who on earth is Clark Anselm?" Carol finally asked.

"Number Three on the F.B.I.'s most-wanted list, that's who," Danforth explained. "The bank robber who blew up the City Savings and Trust in San Francisco four months ago. Killing two people in the process. And escaping scot-free with eighty-some thousand dollars of the bank's money. Mart recognized him from seeing his picture in the newspapers at the time."

"That sweet Calvin Speaker a bank robber?" Helen protested.

"Then why do you suppose he was carrying sixty-seven thousand dollars in cash with him on this cruise?" Leroy asked. "Captain Thorsen had his cabin searched, at our suggestion, and they found big bundles of U.S. currency

"Most of it, anyway," Leroy grinned at his wife. "I also remembered, fortunately, that a reward of five thousand dollars was offered for Clark Anselm's apprehension."

"Whee!" Helen crowed. "Order us another drink, Carol—I think we've just earned ourselves five thousand dollars!"

Danforth shook his head. "Sorry, ladies. The reward is for someone more deserving."

"If you mean who I think you mean, I will join Women's Lib!" said Carol indignantly. "Leroy King?"

"Wrong again," Danforth said. "Gregory. The ship's photographer. He'll get the reward if they take our recommendation. After all, he's the one who really exposed Anselm."

No one laughed at the pun. Helen rocked in her chair as though in pain. "There goes our five thousand dollars!" she moaned. "Excuse me, will you, while I put on my sackcloth dress and throw dust on my head?"

"Forget the dust on the head, darling," advised Leroy. "Remember what happened to Calvin Speaker."

James Holding Bibliography

There is no complete bibliography of stories by James Holding at this time. Shawn Garrett of Wildside helped immensely with this bibliography along with research from various sources and websites.

Novels:

Under the Name of Ellery Queen Jr.
The Mystery of the Merry Magician, Golden Press, 1961.
The Mystery of the Vanished Victim, Golden Press, 1962.
The Purple Bird Mystery, G.P. Putnam's Sons, 1966.

Children's Novels under his own name
The Lazy Little Zulu, William Morrow & Co, Morrow Junior Books, 1962.
Cato the Kiwi Bird, G. P. Putnam's Sons, NY, 1963.
Mr. Moonlight and Omar, E M Hale and Company 1963.
The Mystery of the False Fingertips, Harper & Row, 1964.
Sherlock in Trail, William Morrow & Co, NY, 1964.
The Three Wishes of Hu, G.P. Putnam's Sons, New York, 1965.
Poko and the Golden Demon, Abelard-Schuman, 1968.
The Robber of Featherbed Lane, G.P. Putnam's Sons, New York, 1970.
The Mystery of the Dolphin Inlet, MacMillan, 1968.
A Bottle of Pop, G.P. Putnam's Sons, 1972.
The Watchcat, Xerox Education Publications 1975.
The Ugliest Dog in the World, Xerox Education Publications, 1979.

Short Fiction:

Martin Leroy and King Danforth Series
"The Norwegian Apple Mystery" originally published in *Ellery Queen's Mystery Magazine*, November 1960.
"The African Fish Mystery" originally appeared in *Ellery Queen's Mystery Magazine*, April 1961.
"The Italian Tile Mystery" by James Holding originally appeared in *Ellery Queen's Mystery Magazine*, September 1961.
"The Hong Kong Jewel Mystery" originally appeared in *Ellery Queen's Mystery Magazine*, November 1963.
"The Zanzibar Shirt Mystery" originally appeared in *Ellery Queen's Mystery Magazine*, December 1963.
"The Tahitian Powder Box Mystery" originally appeared in *Ellery Queen's Mystery Magazine*, October 1964.
"The Japanese Card Mystery" originally appeared in *Ellery Queen's Mystery Magazine*, October 1965.
"The New Zealand Bird Mystery" originally appeared in *Ellery Queen's Mystery Magazine*, January 1967.
"The Philippine Key Mystery" originally appeared in *Ellery Queen's Mystery Magazine*, February 1968.
"The Borneo Snapshot Mystery" originally appeared in *Ellery Queen's Mystery Magazine*, January 1972.

Lieutenant Randall Series
"The Vapor Clue" originally appeared in *Alfred Hitchcock Mystery Magazine*, December 1961.
"The Sunburned Fisherman" originally appeared in *Alfred Hitchcock Anthology*, October 1964.
"The Misopedist" originally appeared in *Alfred Hitchcock Mystery Magazine*, April 1968.
"Cause for Alarm" originally appeared in *Ellery Queen's Mystery Magazine*, April 1970.

Manuel Andradas Series
"A Question of Ethics" originally appeared in *Alfred Hitchcock Mystery Magazine*, September 1960.
"The Photographer and the Undertaker" originally appeared in *Ellery Queen's Mystery Magazine*, November 1962.
"The Photographer and the Policeman"originally appeared in *Ellery Queen's Mystery Magazine*, April 1964.
"The Photographer and the Jeweler" originally appeared in *Ellery Queen's Mystery Magazine,* May 1966.
"The Photographer and the Professor" originally appeared in *Ellery Queen's Mystery Magazine,* September, 1966.
"The Photographer and the Columnist" originally appeared in *Ellery Queen's Mystery Magazine*, September 1967.
"The Photographer and the Servant Problem" originally appeared in *Ellery Queen's Mystery Magazine*, October 1970.
"The Photograph and the Artist" originally appeared in *Ellery Queen's Mystery Magazine*, March 1973.
"The Photographer and the Butcher" originally appeared in *Ellery Queen's Mystery Magazine*, July 1973.
"The Photographer and the Jockey originally appeared in *Ellery Queen's Mystery Magazine*, A"ugust 1974.
"The Photographer: Lisbon Assignment" originally appeared in *Ellery Queen's Mystery Magazine*, February 1976.
"The Photographer and the Unknown Victim" originally appeared in *Ellery Queen's Mystery Magazine* April 1976.
"The Photographer and the BLP" originally appeared in *Ellery Queen's Mystery Magazine*, March 1978.
"The Photographer and the Arsonist" originally appeared in *Alfred Hitchcock Mystery Magazine*, November 1980.
"The Photographer and the Letter" originally appeared in *Ellery Queen's Mystery Magazine*, February 1982.
"The Photographer and the Final Payment" originally appeared in *Ellery Queen's Mystery Magazine*, December 1982.
"The Photographer and the Sailor" originally appeared in *Ellery Queen's Mystery Magazine*, March 1984.

Hal Johnson Series

"Library Fuzz" originally appeared in *Ellery Queen's Mystery Magazine* November 1972.

"More Than a Mere Storybook" originally appeared in *Ellery Queen's Mystery Magazine* February 1973.

"The Bookmark" originally appeared in *Ellery Queen's Mystery Magazine* January 1974.

"The Elusive Mrs. Stout" originally appeared in *Ellery Queen's Mystery* Magazine April 1974.

"Hero with a Headache" originally appeared in *Mike Shayne Mystery Magazine*, December 1976.

"Still a Cop" originally appeared in *Ellery Queen's Mystery Magazine* December 1975.

"The Mutilated Scholar" originally appeared in *Ellery Queen's Mystery Magazine* April 1976.

"The Savonarola Syndrome" originally appeared in *Mike Shayne Mystery Magazine*, October 1976.

"The Henchman Case" originally appeared in *Alfred Hitchcock Mystery Magazine,* May 1977.

"The Young Runners" originally appeared in Ellery Queen's Mystery Magazine, July 1978.

"The Honeycomb of Silence" originally appeared in *Alfred Hitchcock's Mystery Magazine,* August 1978.

"The Jack O'Neal Affair" originally appeared in *Alfred Hitchcock's Mystery Magazine*, May 1979.

"The Reward" originally appeared in *Alfred Hitchcock's Mystery Magazine*, October 1980.

"The Search for Tamerlane" originally appeared in *Ellery Queen's Mystery Magazine* May 1981.

"Sideswipe" originally appeared in *Ellery Queen's Mystery Magazine* June 1982.

"The Book Clue" originally appeared in *Ellery Queen's Mystery Magazine* February 1984

Non-series works (listed chronologically)
"The Treasure of Pachacamac" (1960)
"An Accident in Honiora" (1960)
"Go to Sleep, Darling" (1960)
"The Lipstick Explosion" (1960)
"Most Surprised Man in the World" (1960)
"Silent Partner" (1961)
"You Can not Be Too Careful" (1961)
"The Sapphire That Disappeared" (1961)
"Murder's No Bargain" (1961)
"Cotton Cloak, Wood Dagger" (1961)
"No Whitewash for the Doctor" (1961)
"The Stolen Masterpiece" (1961)
"Once Upon a Bank Floor ..." (1961)
"Where Is thy Sting?" (1961)
"Diagnosis: Death" (1961)
"Death in New Zealand" (1961)
"Soft Angel of Mayhem!" (1962)
"Do-It-Yourself Escape Kit" (1962)
"Mexico, With Money" (1962)
"Those Cunning Florentines" (1962)
"The Lost Leopard" (1962)
"Cop Killer" (1962)
"Variation on a Theme" (1963)
"A Mishap in Venice" (1963)
"The Inquisitive Butcher of Nice" (1963)
"Murder of an Unknown Man" (1963)
"Set 'Em Up in the Other Alley" (1963)
"An Exercise in Insurance" (1964)
"Miranda's Lucky Punch" (1964)
"The Spook Goes West" (1964)
"Contraband" (1964)
"Live and Let Live" (1965)
"Career Man" (1965)
"Let the Credit Go" (1965)

"Who Steals My Purse" (1965)
"A Turn to the Right" (1965)
"Death of a Dream" (1966)
"Monkey King" (1966)
"The Proposal" (1966)
"Grounds for Divorce" (1966)
"Suicide Clause" (1966)
"A Felony in the Family" (1966)
"Fly Away Home" (1966)
"No Hiding Place" (1966)
"The Toothpick Murder" (1966)
"The Woman Who Loved Children" (1966)
"The Moonlighter" (1966)
"A Padlock for Charlie Draper" (1967)
"Second Talent" (1968)
"Lesson One" (1968)
"The Dream-Destruction Syndrome" (1968)
"A Steal at the Price" (1969)
"The Dutiful Rookie" (1969)
"A Case of Brotherly Love" (1970)
"Just What the Doctor Ordered" (1970)
'Test Run" (1970)
"Wild Mink" (1970)
"The Consultant" (1970)
"A Good Kid" (1971)
"A Funny Place To Park" (1971)
"Mystery Fan" (1971)
"Conflict of Interest" (1971)
"T'Ang of the Suffering Dragon" (1971)
"A Man Of His Age" (1972)
"The Gambler" (1972)
"A Homemade Dress" (1972)
"Listen to the Dial Tone" (1972)
"A Message From Marsha" (1972)
"Conversation Piece" (1972)
"Hell in a Basket" (1972)

"Weak in the Head" (1973)
"The 1861 Twelve" (1973)
"The Duty of Every Citizen" (1973)
"Hand in Glove" (1973)
"The Montevideo Squeeze" (1973)
"Recipe For Murder" (1973)
"Busman's Holiday" (1974)
"Triple Play" (1974)
"A Visitor To Mombasa" (1971)
"Special Delivery" (1974)
"Your Money or Your Life" (1974)
"The Zamboanga Shuttle" (1974)
"Passport to Paradise" (1974)
"Border Crossing" (1975)
"One Plus One Makes Three" (1975)
"Christian Charity" (1975)
"A Rope Through His Ear" (1975)
"The Fund-Raisers" (1975)
"Break-In" (1976)
"Is There a Doctor in the House?" (1976)
"Beach Party" (1976)
"Rediscovery" (1976)
"In the Soup" (1976)
"The Packing Case" (1976)
"The Blood Tests" (1977)
"Dumb Dude" (1977)
"The Contract" (1977)
"Reason Enough" (1977)
"Open Till Nine" (1978)
"One for the Road" (1978)
"The Swap Shop" (1978)
"The Baby Bit" (1978)
"Paper Caper" (1979)
"The Hummelmeyer Operation" (1979)
"In the Presence of Death" (1979)
"Card Sense" (1979)

"Half a Loaf" (1980)
"Shima Maru" (1981)
"Work of Art"(1981)
"The Only One of Its Kind" (1981)
"By Person or Persons Unknown" (1981)
"Portrait in Yellow" (1981)
"China Trader" (1982)
"A Deal in Rubies" (1982)
"A Decent Price For a Painting" (1982) (Mystery Writers of America Edgar nominee)
"Author! Author!" (1983)
"First Class All the Way" (1983)
"Never Wake a Sleeping Man" (1983)
"A Temporary Bind" (1984)
"Phase Four" (1984)
"The Grave Robber" (1984)
"To His Credit" (1987)
"The Final Deadbeat" (1988)
"Exit the Dragon" (1988)
"The Bank Job" (1988)

The Zanzibar Shirt and Other Stories

The Zanzibar Shirt and Other Stories by James Holding is printed on 60 pound paper, and is designed by Jeffrey Marks, his first for the company, using InDesign. The types are Century Schoolbook and Times New Roman. Century Schoolbook is a transitional serif typeface design by Morris Fuller Benton in 1919. The printing and binding is by Thomson-Shore for the hard cover and the trade paperback version. The book was published in February 2018 by Crippen & Landru Publishers, Inc., Norfolk, VA.

Crippen & Landru, Publishers
P. O. Box 9315
Norfolk, VA 23505
Web: www.Crippenlandru.Com
E-mail: info@crippenlandru.Com

NEW:
Crippen & Landru, Publishers
P. O. Box 532057
Cincinnati, OH 45253

Since 1994, Crippen & Landru has published more than 100 first editions of short-story collections by important detective and mystery writers.

This is the best edited, most attractively packaged line of mystery books introduced in this decade. The books are equally valuable to collectors and readers. [Mystery Scene Magazine]

The specialty publisher with the most star-studded list is Crippen & Landru, which has produced short story collections by some of the biggest names in contemporary crime fiction. [Ellery Queen's Mystery Magazine]

God bless Crippen & Landru. [The Strand Magazine]

A monument in the making is appearing year by year from Crippen & Landru, a small press devoted exclusively to publishing the criminous short story. [Alfred Hitchcock's Mystery Magazine]

Recent Publications

The Columbo Collection by William Link.
New stories written by the creator of television's greatest sleuth. Trade softcover, $18.00.

Ten Thousand Blunt Instruments by Phillip Wylie, edited by Bill Pronzini. Lost Classics Series.
Wylie's stories were, in the words of editor Bill Pronzini, "controversial, provocative, iconoclastic." His detective fiction was among the most ingenious and innovative of his generation. Full cloth with dust jacket, $29.00. Trade softcover, $19.00

The Exploits Of The Patent Leather Kid by Erle Stanley Gardner edited By Bill Pronzini. Lost Classics Series.
The Patent Leather Kid is an elegant crook, hiding his identity with mask, gloves, and shoes made out of black patent leather. In truth, he is a wealthy, seemingly indolent socialite, who becomes a terror to the underworld. Full cloth in dust jacket, $29.00. Trade softcover, $19.00

Valentino: Film Detective by Loren D. Estleman.
Valentino has a perfect job for a film buff – he is a film detective who locates lost movies so that they can be preserved for future generations. And often he has to become an amateur sleuth as well. Full cloth in dust jacket, signed and numbered by the author,
$43.00. Trade softcover, $17.00.

The Duel Of Shadows: The Extraordinary Cases Of Barnabas Hildreth by Vincent Cornier, edited By Mike Ashley. Lost Classics Series.

"One of the great series of modern detective stories." So wrote Ellery Queen when he introduced American readers to the writings of Vincent Cornier. Full cloth in dust jacket, $28.00.

Shooting Hollywood: The Diana Poole Stories by Melodie Johnson Howe.
Melodie Johnson Howe was "one of the last of the starlets," making movies with Clint Eastwood, Alan Alda, James Caan, James Farentino and others. Hollywood is brutal, and it is a place, as Marilyn Monroe said, "where they'll pay you a thousand dollars for a kiss, and fifty cents for your soul ..." Diana Poole finds crime in that world of glitz, glamour, and greed. Full cloth in dust jacket, signed and numbered by the author, $43.00. Trade softcover, $17.00.

The Casebook Of Jonas P. Jonas And Others by E. X. Ferrars, edited By John Cooper. Lost Classics Series.
Stories by a mistress of the traditional mystery. "She remains," wrote one reviewer, "one of the most adept and intelligent adherents of the whodunit form." Full cloth in dust jacket, $29.00. Trade softcover, $19.00.

Nothing Is Impossible: Further Problems Of Dr. Sam Hawthorne by Edward D. Hoch.
Dr. Sam Hawthorne, a New England country doctor in the first half of the twentieth century, was constantly faced by murders in locked rooms and impossible disappearances. *Nothing Is Impossible* contains fifteen of Dr. Sam's most extraordinary cases. Full cloth in dust jacket, signed and numbered by the publisher, $45.00. Trade softcover, $19.00.

Night Call And Other Stories Of Suspense by Charlotte Armstrong, edited By Rick Cypert And Kirby Mccauley. Lost Classics Series.
Charlotte Armstrong introduced suspense into the commonplace, the everyday, by writing short stories and novels in which one simple action sets a series of events spiraling into motion, pulling readers along, breathless with anxiety. Full cloth in dust jacket, $30.00. Trade softcover, $20.00.

Chain Of Witnesses; The Cases Of Miss Phipps by Phyllis Bentley, edited By Marvin Lachman. Lost Classics Series.
A critic writes, "stylistically, [Bentley's] stories ... share a quiet humor and misleading simplicity of statement with the works of Christie .... Her work [is] informed and consistent with the classic traditions of the mystery." Full cloth in dust jacket, $29.00. Trade softcover, $19.00.

Swords, Sandals And Sirens by Marilyn Todd.
Murder, conmen, elephants. Who knew ancient times could be such fun? Many of the stories feature Claudia Seferius, the super-bitch heroine of Marilyn Todd's critically acclaimed mystery series set in ancient rome. Others feature Cleopatra, the olympian gods, and high priestess Ilion blackmailed to work with Sparta's feared secret police. Full cloth in dust jacket, signed and numbered by the author, $45.00. Trade softcover, $19.00.

The Puzzles Of Peter Duluth by Patrick Quentin. Lost Classics Series.
Anthony Boucher wrote: "Quentin is particularly noted

for the enviable polish and grace which make him one of the leading American fabricants of the murderous comedy of manners; but this surface smoothness conceals intricate and meticulous plot construction as faultless as that of Agatha Christie." Full cloth in dust jacket, $29.00. Trade softcover, $19.00.

The Purple Flame And Other Detective Stories by Frederick Irving Anderson, edited By Benjamin F. Fisher. Previously uncollected stories by one of the premier mystery writers of the 1920's and the 1930's. Full cloth in dust jacket, $29.00. Trade softcover, $19.00.

My Mother, The Detective: The Complete "Mom" Stories by James Yaffe. Second edition enlarged. Trade softcover, $19.00

All But Impossible: The Impossible Files of Dr. Sam Hawthorne by Edward D. Hoch. Full cloth in dust jacket, signed and numbered by the publisher, $45.00. Trade softcover, $19.00.

Subscriptions

Subscribers agree to purchase each forthcoming publication, either the Regular Series or the Lost Classics or (preferably) both. Collectors can thereby guarantee receiving limited editions, and readers won't miss any favorite stories.

Subscribers receive a discount of 20% off the list price (and the same discount on our backlist) and a specially commissioned short story by a major writer in a deluxe edition as a gift at the end of the year.

The point for us is that, since customers don't pick and choose which books they want, we have a guaranteed sale even before the book is published, and that allows us to be more imaginative in choosing short story collections to issue.

That's worth the 20% discount for us. Sign up now and start saving. Email us at crippenlandru@earthlink.net or visit our website at www.crippenlandru.com on our subscription page.